Contents

WINTER SUN

A finalist in the 2020 Irish Novel Fair.

Miki Lentin took up writing while travelling the world with his family a few years ago. He completed an MA in Creative Writing at Birkbeck in 2020 and was a finalist in the 2020 Irish Novel Fair. He has been placed highly in competitions including the Fish Publishing Short Memoir Prize 2020, Brick Lane Bookshop New Short Stories 2022 and Leicester Writes, and published in *Litro*, *MIR* and other publications. His collection of short stories *Inner Core* was published by Afsana Press in 2022. *Winter Sun* is his debut novel. Miki dreams of one day running a literary café.

For more information, you can visit:
www.mikilentin.net/my-writing

"Bittersweet, funny and tender, *Winter Sun* is about the mysterious relationship between parent and adult child, the fragility of the ageing body, the strangeness of family holidays and the comforts of alcohol and literature. You can't help falling in love with Miki and Abba, willing them on to find a common language—and ideally a whiskey they can both agree on."

Viv Groskop, author of *The Anna Karenina Fix*

"Written from the heart, with skill and honesty, this is a warm, highly intelligent novel. Just beautiful. I was thoroughly moved by *Winter Sun*. An elegantly constructed, moving and hilarious read that brings the reader to Tenerife, the Hotel Optimist and home again, with some elegant twists and thought provoking questions about how we love each other, and how maybe imperfect love is love enough. A page turner!"

Niamh Boyce, author of *The Herbalist* and *Her Kind*

"A gentle, finely crafted novel with a brilliantly realised father-son relationship, and a nuanced, beautifully written observation of old age. It's fitting our narrator reads Saul Bellow in this book, because for me, Lentin's achievement in *Winter Sun* sits alongside Bellow's in *Seize the Day*; they both create such a memorable and vivid rendering of a father-son relationship in adulthood."

Kevin Curran, author of *Youth*, *Citizens* and *Beatsploitation*.

WINTER SUN

Miki Lentin

Afsana Press
London

First published in 2024

by Afsana Press Ltd, London

www.afsana-press.com

Winter Sun is a work of fiction. Although it contains real, historical events and mentions of real personalities, all characters, places, events, organisations and institutions in this novel are either products of the author's imagination or are used fictitiously.

Typeset by Afsana Press Ltd

Printed and bound by CPI Group (UK) Ltd, Croydon, CR0 4YY

A CIP catalogue record for this book

is available from the British Library

ISBN: 978-1-7399824-9-2

For Miriam

June 30, 1992, Dublin

Dear Maestro,

Your wonderful letter arrived yesterday,
and what a wonderful letter it is! Let me
say right now that I think it is full of
feeling, concern and humanity, just what I
would expect you to come up with. I am so
pleased that you sent me your poems, it's
something I was never able to do with my
father. Your mother is still away, so I'm
writing this after a marvellous meal that
damn well cost me a small fortune, but
luckily they allowed me to take what was
left of the bottle home, which I'm knocking
off as I write you…

This was the last holiday I went on with my father.

Steak Tartare

Friday, December 12, 2006

The 08:20 flight from Dublin to Tenerife was delayed. A cold breeze circulated with the hot air of the cabin as we waited for the doors to close, the seat belt sign to ping on, and the relief of the aeroplane to push back.

My father, who I called Abba, father in Hebrew, dozed next to me in the aisle seat of row twelve. Now in his mid-seventies, he craved an annual dose of winter sun, hoping it would help relieve him of his *tzores*, troubles. My mother usually accompanied him on his pilgrimage to the Canary Islands. This year, she refused to go. I protested that I had better things to do, and suggested that he enjoyed his own company, so couldn't he just go alone? But she insisted. She needed me to look after him. She told me he enjoyed my company. I was between jobs. I didn't really have anything else on, so finally agreed to be his chaperone.

Abba had removed his sandals and socks exposing his calloused feet and stretched out his legs. A muscle man sat in the window seat, bulky headphones on his head, his sharp elbow occupying the armrest to my left. I was squashed tight, in the middle.

Earlier, Abba had insisted that it was too far to walk to

the departure gate, so I booked the airport buggy. The driver and other passengers though weren't amused by his frequent toilet stops and detour through Duty Free to pick up a bottle of Jameson's whiskey, where he also took the liberty of tasting a single malt that he managed to spill onto his smock. While he was drinking, I knocked over a bottle of aftershave with my backpack, an edge of the thick transparent glass chipping on the ground. No-one seemed to notice and pretending it wasn't me, I kicked the splinter of glass under a counter, replaced the bottle on the shelf and re-joined Abba on the buggy. I told myself the damage was nothing as the buggy drove away, but the bottle was chipped, on the edge, a bit like me.

Half an hour after taking our seats, gusts of wind lifted the aeroplane through icy drizzle over Dublin Bay into heavy clouds, leaving my empty stomach behind. Abba laid his warm hand on mine, his wedding ring resting firmly on my knuckle. I closed my eyes, pushed my head back against the headrest, and wondered when it had last been cleaned of other people's greasy hair. With every shudder the aeroplane made, I pulled my seat belt tighter, gripped the armrests and repeatedly read the instructions on the safety card that was laminated onto the back of the seat in front. How would I get Abba out in an emergency, I wondered. In his state, there was no way he'd be able to scramble through the cabin aisle to safety. Would I just leave him, alone, waiting to be rescued?

Ten minutes later, the seat belt sign chimed off. I climbed over Abba, went to the bathroom, and looked at myself in the backlit mirror. He often moaned that my posture was curved and that I should see his "marvellous" Feldenkrais practitioner who would put me right.

I stretched my shoulders back until I stood straight, but they quickly sprung forward, as if my body preferred to hunch. My eyes were bloodshot and eyelids baggy behind my glasses. My forehead was creased with concern. I tried to freshen up by splashing some water onto my unkempt beard and running my wet hand over my balding head, but the tautness in my face remained.

A bout of turbulence shook the aeroplane, so I sat on the closed toilet seat in the cramped cubicle, one hand clutching the handrail until it passed. Rummaging through my wallet, I removed a piece of lined A5 paper I'd been meaning to look at. The sharp folds had nearly worn through the fibres, so I unfolded it carefully, stared at my messy handwriting, and silently read five questions I'd brought to ask Abba while we were away. I caught a few glimpses of how I might ask these questions; maybe over dinner, or during a drive, but the thoughts faded quickly. I was left thinking nothing much, apart from an image of my Imma, mother in Hebrew, waving at the taxi earlier that morning as we drove away from my parents' house in Harold's Cross in Dublin in the dark.

Breathing deeply, I delicately folded the piece of paper and slid it back into my wallet, wiped the sink with a paper towel, and listened to the suds get sucked into the bowels of the fuselage.

These days Abba just about tolerated flying. "If I must," he'd say, like he was doing me a favour. "But what's wrong with a good ferry?" He'd often recount tales of what he called "civilised travel," in the 1950s and 60s. Long days of reading in the sun, usually Joyce, Bellow or Roth, eating steak for breakfast on the

QEII to New York, and black-tie dinners accompanied by a string quartet. He'd recall that for two shillings and six-pence, you could get a drink and a "pleasant" meal at Dublin Airport before flying to London in luxury. Now, there was nowhere to have a "decent" cup of coffee and the pubs were crowded with "yobbos" watching football. There was none of this queueing and "security nonsense" that he blamed on the IRA.

Back in my seat, I studied this man I'd known for thirty-five years. His pond-like eyes were closed behind his square rimmed bifocals. He'd taken off his corduroy flat cap, exposing blood blisters that dotted his bald head. A crescent of tightly shaved white hair ran around the back of his skull. His teeth, Sellotape yellow, were visible behind his chapped lips that were ajar. Two shaving scabs hung loosely on his bristly neck, which sagged like elbow skin. He refused to trim the twisted vines of his eyebrows that sprouted in all directions, possibly proud that something was still growing. Every so often, he'd reach under his smock, rub his grapefruit-sized hernia that protruded from the side of his abdomen, and hold it, like he was carrying an extra limb.

I nudged Abba awake as the drinks trolley arrived. The flight attendant raised her eyebrows at me. Her name Ludmila was embossed on a badge clipped onto her synthetic shirt.

Abba stretched his arms above his head. "A little whiskey?" he asked.

"We've got Bullseye, Irish whiskey. It's four for two this morning," Ludmila said, her accent Eastern European.

"We'll take four."

"It's a bit early, don't you think?" I asked.

"To hell with it. Come on. Join me."

Ludmila dropped four squidgy sachets of Bullseye onto the tray table in front of me and passed me a coffee.

Abba found a twenty euro note among his boarding pass, credit card and tattered pacemaker document in the back pocket of his trousers and paid. While trying to rip open the sachets he muttered to me that this was all very well and good, but what was wrong with "good, old fashioned bottles", to which the muscle man nodded his agreement. Unable to tear open the sachets, he threw one at me and suggested that I have a go. I bit the corner of one and squeezed half the liquid into a glass that shook in his hand, with the rest spraying onto his trousers and hitting my wrist. Abba dabbed the wet patch with a corner of his frayed handkerchief, where I spotted his initials LL crookedly embroidered in green thread. I recollected sewing the letters for him as a birthday present, hoping he'd use it for special occasions, but it ended up like all his other handkerchiefs, greying and stained.

"Is that all you're taking?" I'd asked Abba the night before we left as I helped him pack his suitcase.

"Sure I only need one pair of trousers."

"And what if they get dirty?"

"Otherwise I'll just have to carry more. You can always do laundry in the hotel, can't you?"

"Can I now?" I mumbled. As well as his few items of clothing, I stuffed into his suitcase his beloved blue towelling dressing gown, a hard-back copy of Stefan Zweig's *The World of Yesterday*, Isaac Bashevis Singer's *The Slave*, a theatre script he wanted to read, a list of prescription medication from his doctor, his favoured sunscreen Piz Buin, flip-flops so over-used that the heel had nearly worn through, sandals with Velcro straps, a bucket sun hat and a black medicine kit that was jammed with different coloured pots of pills, tubes of foot emollient, Insulin vials, anti-constipation powders, vitamins A, D and E, plasters, a Wilkinson Sword razor and blades, Shavex, nail file, menthol dental floss and, his Solpadeines. He didn't take his camera.

"*L'Chaim*, cheers," Abba said, raising his glass. "Thanks for coming."

"*L'Chaim*… Jesus," I said, sputtering on the acrid whiskey that ripped some skin from the roof of my mouth.

I emptied the remaining sachets of whiskey into our glasses, leaving them lying in a sodden heap on a paper towel.

The aeroplane dipped its wing, filling the windows with brilliant blue sky. I took the *Berlitz Pocket Guide to Tenerife* out of my backpack and looked for things for Abba and me to do, places to visit, restaurants to eat at, but the print was small, the layout confusing, the map code difficult to decipher. After a few pages my eyelids grew heavy and I lost interest, but the incessant tinkle from the headphones of the man next to me kept me awake. I flicked aimlessly through a well-thumbed in-flight magazine, spotting a feature about the Aran Islands off the west coast of Ireland, and thought of the last holiday I'd been on with Abba.

In my early twenties, Abba invited me to accompany him on a New Year's weekend to Inishmore, the largest of the Aran Islands. "Go with him", my mother pleaded, "he loves spending time with you." I wondered what I would say when my friends asked me what I did on the biggest night of the year? But I didn't have any other plans, and the thought of staying at home and watching the *Late Late Show* didn't appeal.

Of course Abba knew the right place to stay, a youth hostel, owned by a former opera singer he'd met producing a television series on the best places to stay and eat across Ireland. Our bedroom, painted purple, was draughty and damp, the single mattresses unyielding, the sheets scratchy and blankets heavy. Brown water stains clouded the ceiling of our room, and outside rusty cigarette bins overflowed with sodden butts. He forgot that the hostel only served vegetarian food.

There was little to do on the island apart from read, sleep and walk. We'd usually head to the cliffs of Dun Aengus fort, neither of us saying much as our boots crunched on the rocky paths. Scrambling on our fronts, we liked to dangle our heads over the cliff edges and watch the herons and seagulls swoop through the spray into the sea for fish, our bodies vibrating as the Atlantic Ocean pounded the rock-face like a drum.

Sometimes we'd stop to take photographs of derelict cottages, split Karst limestone and silhouettes of ancient standing stones with Abba's manual Yashica SLR camera, often experimenting with different lenses and filters. Forever the television director, he'd point and demand that I grab the shot "quickly", or I'd miss the light. When he spotted a shot he wanted to take, I'd stand behind him and wrap my arms around his body to steady his shaking hands as he clicked and rolled on the film.

Every so often, horizontal driving rain would sweep in from the Atlantic, clouds racing across the sky. Despite my pleas to head back to the hostel, my eyes watery and ears painfully red, Abba would insist that we shelter against a drystone wall, gales blowing up our waterproof jackets like balloons.

"I'd love to live here," he said, cradling a whiskey in a pub one afternoon after a walk.

"What would you do?" I asked.

"Sit, read, not talk to anyone," he laughed.

"Don't be ridiculous, you'd be bored stiff."

Abba took a long gulp of his drink and wiped his mouth with the back of his hand. "Forget it, I didn't think you'd understand."

I spent New Year's Eve making vacuous conversation with an elderly couple and picked at smoked salmon blinis and plates of cheese. Abba sat quietly and swirled red wine around his glass, a semi-satisfied smile on his stained lips.

"You OK?" I'd ask him every few minutes.

"I'm fine. Why do you keep asking?"

The owner of the hostel led arias from *West Side Story* and *The Threepenny Opera* to laughter and applause. After a few songs, Abba asked a woman of a similar age to dance. I followed his movements in a mirror, one hand holding hers, the other lightly clasping her waist, their bloated bodies swaying to the music. At midnight, he kissed the woman lightly on her cheek, gave her a squeeze, whispered something in her ear and winked at me. I gazed at him through a shower of streamers and balloons and for a few seconds wondered if I should say something, ask him what he was doing. But he'd probably tell me to "relax" and "mind my own bloody business". I decided to leave him be. After all, he seemed to be enjoying himself and wasn't that what we all wanted for him? Soon after 'Auld Lang Syne' I went to bed without saying good night. We travelled home the next day, neither of us speaking.

An hour into the flight, Abba removed a copy of Philip Roth's *Everyman* from the pocket of his smock and started to read.

"How's Roth?" I asked.

"Marvellous," he said, using one of his favourite words that he always pronounced languidly with his eyes closed, as if he was in a momentary dreamlike state.

"What's it about?"

"A Jewish man who's dealing with old age I suppose." He paused. "Look, before you say anything, I adore Roth. I don't care what the bloody feminists say." This was how it began. "Your mother absolutely refuses to read any of his books. She won't even try."

"I don't think it's her kind of thing."

"I don't give a damn if it's not her 'kind of thing', there's no harm in trying."

I sighed.

"I'll borrow it when you're done and tell you what I think," I said.

"I'll buy you a copy."

"Can't you just lend me yours?"

"I like to have my own," he insisted.

It was a pointless discussion. Every so often, I'd surreptitiously borrow one of Abba's books and take it back with me to London. He'd quickly discover a gap in the shelf, as if he'd catalogued the location of every book he owned. There'd be a phone call on the landline, and a demand for a postal return. I'd refuse, jokingly, but now and again he'd remind me like a strict librarian of the items that were overdue. Reluctantly, I'd agree.

As the plane descended, Abba drank some water from a plastic bottle that I held to his lips so it wouldn't spill. Unbuckling his seat belt he stood up.

"Please. Sir," Ludmila said, running up to him, "you need to sit down, we'll be landing in a few minutes."

"I have to go to the bathroom!"

"Sir!" she said firmly, "the Captain has switched on the seat belt sign. You have to sit down."

"Cabin crew, five minutes," the Captain announced.

Abba lent on the back of the seat in front to steady himself, pushed past Ludmila and shuffled down the aisle in his bare feet.

When he returned, I noticed his khaki drawstring trousers were darker at the crotch.

The aeroplane landed with a thump a few minutes later, and sped along a runway surrounded by a landscape of scorched grass and palm trees.

"Ahhh, the sun, finally. Beats the bloody weather at home," Abba said, his bifocals darkening in the blistering sunlight as we stood at the top of the steps to the aeroplane. He hooked his arm around mine. We descended towards the tarmac one step at a time, and boarded a stuffy bus.

"Christ, it's hot in here," Abba said, and started to take off his smock.

"What are you doing?" I whispered.

He ignored me, and continued to remove his smock as his book, sachets of Solpadeine and a used insulin vial fell out of the pockets. I helped him lift it off, exposing his hairy chest

16

and breasts that drooped out of the side of his vest. Some of the other passengers gawked at him. One parent pulled away a child that stood too close, and another shook her head. I thought of wrapping him up in his smock, but instead, placed an arm around his shoulders and held him tight.

"Two drivers?" the Assistant asked at the Hertz car hire desk.

"Yes please," Abba responded.

"Just one," I interrupted, and quickly initialled the forms for a Cinquecento.

"I can drive you know."

"I know…"

We drove along a dual carriageway towards the resort of Playa de las Américas, on the southern tip of the island. At some stage during the drive, he explained to me in detail that it was great that the car had no electric windows, and that he hated electric windows, as you couldn't open them just a tad, and what was wrong with a perfectly good old-fashioned design, and why did things have to change all the time, and the reason he hadn't had the electric windows on his car at home fixed was because the parts weren't available and anyway, it would cost two hundred euros to fix, so my mother and him would have to drive with a closed window for the time being until the parts came in from Japan, and he hated driving with the windows closed, and so a manual window handle would have been a much better idea all along. I only half listened.

Located in the centre of town, the Hotel Optimist was surrounded by a couple of high-rise office blocks and a supermarket. Palm trees sent long afternoon shadows over an oval swimming pool in a central courtyard. Flecks of white paint scattered the pavement outside reception, and inside a smell of pungent aftershave filled the lobby. A set of digital LED clocks showing the time in Tenerife, Dublin and New York hung on the wall behind the welcome desk. We waited to be served.

"Eh, excuse me," a man behind us said.

Abba and I turned.

Somewhere in his late-twenties, his eyes were hidden behind round reflective sunglasses. He was wearing a 'Sun-Seeker Holidays' sleeveless t-shirt with 'Here to Help' printed on the front, a baseball cap, knee-length football shorts and sliders. His skin glowed sunbed orange.

"Are you the…" he said, running his finger down a clipboard, "Lentons?"

"Lentins," Abba said curtly.

"That's us," I said.

"You had me worried there for a while. I thought you'd gone home or something. I waited for you and you at the airport," he said, pointing at Abba and me. "You delayed the coach," he said accusingly. "I was told you were getting the bus with everyone else."

"We hired a car," I said.

"Sure you don't need a car around here. Everything you need is here, in Playa," he said, opening up his arms.

"I'm not sitting here all day," Abba said, sniffing loudly, "I need to get some sun."

"You'll get loads of sun here, it's been lovely and hot today."

"I need the bathroom. What room are we in?" Abba asked.

"I've put you in the mini apartment, three, zero, four," he said handing me two key cards. "Listen," he continued, "let me know if you plan to go off somewhere, OK? While you're here you're my responsibility. I have a duty of care and all that, health and safety you know." He paused. "Are you joining us for dinner?"

I started to back away, keeping one eye on Abba who was walking towards the lift.

"It's Mexican night tonight," the man continued, "so you get two chicken fajitas for the price of one, and they throw in a few shrimp. Oh, and then there's karaoke. Do you like singing?"

"We'll, eh, think about it."

"Well if you need anything, ask for me, Richard." He held out his hand, and as he squashed my fingers I noticed a gold cross hanging from his neck, and the name Mary tattooed on his shoulder.

The carpet of the apartment was threadbare, the walls magnolia, the pendants dusty. A thick smell of furniture polish filled the air, as if it was trying to mask another odour. The tabletop fridge in the kitchen gurgled, and a red light blinked on the telephone.

"Meh. The agent told me there'd be a view," Abba said, looking out of his bedroom window.

"Of what?" I asked from the lounge that was filled with a leather sofa and a low coffee table.

"A view, a view. You know, something to look at, the sea perhaps. The place I booked last year for your mother and me had a view."

"Well, I can see a supermarket and the car park," I shouted from my room, drawing the heavy curtains.

Abba spent some time unpacking, neatly arranging his books on his bedside table. I dumped my bag in the corner of my room, preferring to leave it unpacked.

Sometime later, he leant against the frame of my bedroom door and stretched his arms wide. "I'm whacked," he declared, "I'm going for a snooze. Wake me up when it's time for dinner."

Sitting on the tiled balcony that faced onto the swimming pool, I opened my book, lit a cigarette and downed two paracetamol, enjoying the sugar coating of the tablets. A few holidaymakers had crammed their sun loungers into a corner of the pool area, offering their already seared bodies to the last rays of sun for the day.

Over the past few months, I'd been picking my way through Abba's copy of Saul Bellow's *Herzog*. The cover, creased and frayed at the edges, had a picture of a scrunched-up ball of paper with messy handwriting and was inscribed with the words, 'the half-drunk author, best wishes, Saul Bellow' from a book signing Abba had attended some years before.

Every time I opened it, I couldn't help but think of a conversation I'd had with my shrink. Week after week for the past few months, I'd sit in her chintzy living room, in semi-darkness on a sunken couch that was matted with cat hair. Her coffee was instant, the milk sometimes off, her shelves filled with the spines of books such as *I'm OK – You're OK* and *Staying OK*. I was there to talk about Abba and me, but often said nothing, until I told her one week that I had agreed to accompany him on holiday and was reading *Herzog*.

"It's an interesting choice of book to read," she said, looking at me over her glasses, smiling ponderously, bits of parsley stuck between her teeth. It was the first time she'd smiled at me, as if she knew that I was only reading *Herzog* to impress Abba, to give us something to talk about, to distract us.

I shrugged.

"Are you enjoying it?" she asked.

"Suppose."

"If you're not enjoying it, then why are you reading it?"

I didn't respond.

"There's no harm in stopping you know."

I sank into the couch knowing she was right, but there was something about *Herzog*'s ramblings, disconnected obsessions and letter writing that made me want to continue.

It was no longer day as we sat on high stools in the crowded hotel bar. A group of men huddled together watching a *La Liga* football match on a plasma screen. Children ran amongst parents' legs, and families gathered around tall bar tables littered with packets of crisps.

"Shall we do *Shabbat*?" Abba asked.

"Here?"

"*Lama lo*, why not?"

"It's not exactly the right place, is it?" A man reached over me to pay for a pint. "With what anyway?"

"I don't know, whiskey, and maybe you can find a box of matches."

"Can't we just take a break from it?" I sighed.

"It's Friday night. I'd like to do *Shabbat*."

Reluctantly, I ordered two Jameson's and a bowl of spiced cashews from the barman, and asked if I could borrow a cigarette lighter. Abba and I stood against the bar. I sparked the lighter, held it high in my hand, and began to mumble the *shabbat* blessing for lighting the candles.

"*Baruch, ato Adonai, elohenu melech…*"

"Hey, *señor*, no smoking," the barman said, pointing to a sign above the bar. His name, Raul, was sewn onto his sleeveless shirt. As he spoke, a gold front tooth shone in the spotlights, and a scar glistened on the side of his face.

"Oh, no, sorry, it's for a prayer, you know, *Shabbat*. God, how do I? God, you know… God, we're Jewish," I said, pointing to a Star of David hanging from my neck.

"Oh, OK, but no smoking."

Raul stopped to shine a glass and studied us from behind the bar as I blessed the whiskey and sanctified the nuts. We drank, and Abba started to belt out the hymn *Le Cha Do-Di* at the top of his voice.

"Do we *have* to sing?" I interrupted him.

Abba continued, getting the Hebrew all wrong. After a verse, I joined in, if only to help him with the words, and sang along while staring at my drink. For a brief moment, he stopped itching and rubbing his hernia. His hands were still, his voice clear.

As we finished singing, I felt a tap on my shoulder. I turned and in front of me was a woman with a peeling forehead.

"Hi," I said.

"I just wanted to say that I think it's great that you're singing with your dad in Irish. What song was it?"

"What song was it?" I asked confused. "Oh, no, we were signing in Hebrew."

"Oh, is that like Jewish?"

"Yeh, well, it's the language that Jews, I mean, it's the Jewish language I suppose. We use it for prayers."

"So what are you doing singing?"

"It's *Shabbat*, Friday night, I mean the Sabbath, so we sing songs, you know, to celebrate."

"Oh. Well. Lovely. That's lovely. Ahem, nice to meet you, and your dad." She scurried back to her table, and whispered to a young girl who was digging her hand into a pot of Pringles.

Abba wiggled his finger at Raul.

"*Señor*," Raul said.

"Where's decent to eat around here? I feel like a good steak."

"Try the Vegas Grill. You go to the main road and up the hill. You'll see the sign. It's easy to find *amigo*."

I felt like driving fast, longing to enjoy the warm evening breeze on my bare arms, but the Cinquecento struggled to get up the steep hill.

"For God's sake, don't leave it in third," Abba said.

I pressed the accelerator to the floor. The car didn't respond.

"Your mother always leaves it in third."

Night fell as I parked the car. A man singing *The Wild Rover* carried in the wind. A sweet tropical smell emanated from jasmine and bougainvillea bushes that covered the entrance to the restaurant. The singing got louder as we entered the open-air space, lit up with signs of Las Vegas hotels. Long tables were tightly packed with holidaymakers who wore bright shirts and tops that glowed like fluorescent light bulbs against their tanned skin.

A waitress gestured for us to follow her. We walked around the front of the stage to a table by the side of the dance floor.

"This OK?" I asked Abba as we sat down.

"Ah, it will do," Abba said, as he cleaned his glasses with the corner of his shirt.

"We can go somewhere else if you'd like," I shouted over the music.

"*Ze beseder*, it's fine," he said, flicking through the extensive leather-bound menu.

The waitress returned with a basket of bread.

Groups of diners sang in unison, swaying from side to side, bingo-wings wrapped around each other's shoulders.

"Two steak tartares," Abba declared.

"What?" I asked.

"Come on, your mother doesn't cook red meat anymore, it's my treat. Ah, wait, has the meat been hung?" Abba looked up at the waitress.

"*Señor*?"

"Hung. All meat should be hung."

She looked at me quizzically.

"Abba, I don't think she understands," I shouted.

"Hung, you know, hung," Abba said. He pushed his hands into the table and stood up while grabbing his napkin in his fist. He lifted his arm high, bent his head, opened his mouth wide, stuck out his tongue and closed his eyes. "Hung," he cried, startling a few other guests on the next table.

"For God's sake, sit down," I said.

"I'll ask the chef, OK?" the waitress said.

"Relax, it's just a little joke," he said, sitting down. "To hell with it. I'm sure it'll be fine."

The music stopped for a while. The waitress returned and mixed the raw minced beef with capers, shallots, Tabasco, chopped gherkins, salt, pepper and a raw egg. She dolloped it onto our plates. Abba tucked into his helping, but quickly reached over and dug his fork into my plate of food. We picked at the meat that was tough and had a sour tang, as if it had recently been defrosted in a microwave. As he ate, Abba raised his wine glass to his mouth using both hands, but couldn't avoid a few drops sprinkling his shirt like tiny specks of blood.

"Welcome back, the one and only, Irish Amigos," an announcer bellowed through a microphone.

"Thank you," the lead singer said and started singing *Suspicious Minds*. The crowd joined in loudly.

"Shall we go?" I asked, but Abba palmed his hand up and down, one of his signals that he was in no rush. He settled back into his chair and continued to swirl his wine around his glass as we knocked off a bottle of Merlot. I watched a few couples dance, thousands of sparkles reflecting from a disco ball onto them as they swung their tubby bodies, kissed and laughed with wide grins and snuggled up to each other's necks. At some stage Abba went off to pee and bumped into a couple, knocking them slightly off balance, and for a split second I thought I'd have to retrieve him from an altercation with another man he'd bumped into, but he quickly disappeared through the strobe lights towards the bathroom. Waiting for Abba to return, I tore at the label on the bottle of wine with my nails, the paper curling and sticking to my fingers.

*

Later that night, I saw Abba through a gap in the door to his bedroom sitting on the edge of his bed in his vest and y-fronts. He swallowed a few tablets with a glass of water. When I was six, I'd unlock his medicine cabinet that hung on our bathroom wall and steal his various pills. I hid them in my rabbit hand puppet which I left under my pillow. The clear ones, where I could see the contents, were my favourites. Every time I pinched another pill, I counted my collection and wrote down the number on a piece of paper I kept. Eventually, I'd gathered more than thirty. My mother found them one night and screamed. I promised my parents I hadn't taken any. I told them I wanted to be a man, like Abba.

"*Laila tov*, good night," I whispered.

"*Laila tov* maestro," he said, briefly raising his head to me. He hardly ever called me that anymore.

I sat on the balcony, lit a cigarette and tried to read *Herzog* in the dim overhead light, but couldn't concentrate. A mosquito buzzed around my ear. There was a chill in the air. The laughter and yelps from the karaoke drifted across the wind from the hotel bar. I vacantly watched a few people jump and push each other into the pool, big lads doing cannonballs and girls following them with sparkly sandals still strapped to their feet.

Instead of coming on holiday, maybe I should have taken Abba out for a meal in Dublin to discuss my questions. I pondered this as I inhaled deeply on one cigarette after another, extinguishing the burnt tobacco onto the brickwork of next door's balcony. I tried to remember what I'd written on my piece of paper, but for some reason all I could think about was the shard of glass that I'd kicked under the counter in Duty Free. I wondered if someone would cut themselves on the chipped bottle of after-shave, and for a brief moment I saw a person with a bleeding thumb remonstrate with the check-out assistant that a bottle they'd taken off a shelf had split their skin and they were bleeding, they had a plane to catch and for god's sake where was the first aid kit and why was a broken bottle on the shelf anyway, and did they know that they had a holiday to get to and now their clothes were stained with blood and who was going to pay for the dry cleaning, and that would be my fault. But it was done. I was here. On holiday with Abba.

…I should have said at the beginning that I was typing this so that you could read my handwriting. I'm tempted to leave in all the typing mistakes, but then the mystery in between some of the lines would be too obscure. Your descriptions of your adventures in China are fascinating, and I look forward to hearing everything from you when you get home. It's funny how many people I know and now you, who have gone to parts of China have liked it and I can just picture you at the Great Wall! Anyway, China or no China, I envy you lying on beaches and eating all that great food. No doubt you'll come back looking great from your trip, well, you always do. I notice a reference to a new friend… one at a time… please…

DAY TWO

The Germans

I fell into a canal when I was a toddler and nearly drowned. I pushed a dingy away from the edge of a bank and followed it into the water. There was never any danger, or so I'd been led to believe from the countless times I'd heard Abba recount the story of how I was fished out by one of his playwright friends. I have no memory of what happened. Was the water still and cold? Was I wearing the strawberry hat that I seemed to wear a lot at that age? Did I float face down? Were there ducks in the canal? Was the sky grey? Did I drift or get tangled in the reeds? Did time pause? The images of that day have never sharpened, but that morning in the Hotel Optimist when lying half asleep in bed, as often happens, I thought I felt a heavy arm reach around my body and pull me abruptly out of the water, my clothes dripping, my hat sodden over my eyes, my skin icy and me, coming too, bewildered.

The shadowy feeling of being rescued continued to shudder through me as I looked out onto the hotel pool from a table in the refectory-like breakfast room. A lifeguard was trailing a net across the water's surface, collecting leaves and deflated plastic toys left over from the day before. Being a lifeguard looked like an easy life; endless days of swimming, reading and sitting in the sun. Maybe it could be my next job? If called into action, maybe I'd pull someone out of the water alive, maybe I'd be the hero, maybe the story would be about me.

"Ah! There you are," Abba said, startling me.

"*Boker tov*, good morning."

I moistened a corner of a paper napkin in a glass of water, leant towards him and dabbed a shaving cut on his cheek. He took it from me, pressed it against the cut and let a trickle of watery blood dribble down his neck.

A few breakfast stragglers appeared in their slippers, hair still wet, wrapped in hotel dressing gowns. I grabbed Abba and I some toast, natural yoghurt and a bowl of limp watermelon. As I picked at the food, Abba tried to force open a plastic pot of pills for his daily dose of medication with his teeth until the lid flew open, and blue and red pills scattered across the Formica table and onto the floor like hailstones.

"Shit!" Abba cried.

I gathered the pills that had landed on the table.

"What are they?" I asked.

"Painkillers, for my feet, and this nasty thing," he said, patting his hernia. "Do me a favour and pick those up," he said pointing to the floor.

"No chance, it's filthy."

"Suit yourself, but I may not have enough now, so it's either that, or it's a trip to the pharmacy," he said, shrugging his shoulders.

I bent down to get under the table and got onto all fours, my hands sliding on spilt coffee and bits of cereal that stuck to my bare knees. Reaching along the skirting boards, I collected as many pills as I could. Just before I stretched for the last one,

I accidentally brushed the leg of another hotel guest who was sitting next to us with my hand.

"What was that?" the man cried. His leg flinched.

A man with a mullet poked his head under the table.

"Sorry," I said.

"Are you feeling my leg?"

"No," I mumbled.

"It wasn't anyone else, was it?"

"What's going on down there?" I heard a woman ask.

"Nothing," he said.

"Sorry, I didn't mean to, eh," I said, lifting my head. "I'm just picking these up for my father." I showed him the pills. "I'll only be a sec. Got it."

"What did he say?" the same woman asked.

"Something about picking up some pills."

"Tell him to stop."

"I did," he rubbed the back of his leg.

I sat back down and enjoyed the feeling of blood rushing down from my head, making me momentarily dizzy. Brushing the dirt from my hands and legs I carefully funnelled the pills into their pot, holding two back in my hand.

"Good man," Abba said.

"You're welcome," I said begrudgingly, trying not to catch the eye of the man next to us.

"Did you sleep well?" Abba asked after a few minutes.

"Not bad."

"Well, we'd be better off sleeping in than getting up for this breakfast." Abba sniffed loudly, curling his upper lip to his nostrils.

"I wake up at five thirty every morning, so it doesn't really matter."

"How long has that been going on for?"

"A few years."

"I've always been an insomniac," Abba declared, as if he was the only person who suffered from a lack of sleep.

"You've told me."

"My feet are so hot they keep me awake most of the night. Have I told you what the doc calls it?"

I nodded.

"Restless leg syndrome. Tell you what, it is a bloody syndrome. RLS. And before you ask, there's nothing I can take for it."

"What's it like?"

"As if my legs are constantly running away from me. It's infuriating."

"Why don't you go for a walk or something?"

"In the middle of the night? Are you mad?"

He paused.

"You know what I do?" he said, edging a little closer. "I make a little cocktail. Two Solps and a little whiskey. Don't tell your mother. Knocks me out. Every time."

"I'm sure it does." I shook my head.

"God, I'd do anything for a decent night's sleep," he yawned.

I nodded, glanced at the two pills in my hand, and stuffed them into the pocket of my shorts.

We took our coffees and sat on a couple of plastic chairs by the pool and watched eager sun-seekers unroll their beach towels onto loungers, lather themselves with sun cream, lie down, and wait for the sun to emerge. Still crumpled, my shorts felt stiff from the wash and rubbed against my thighs. A t-shirt label scratched the back of my neck. Abba was wearing the only shorts he'd brought. Blood blisters glistened on his hairless calves and thighs. His brittle toenails, thick and ingrained with fungus were outgrowing his toes. He refused to treat them, saying that he'd tried all the nail creams, varnishes, oils and pills he could get his hands on. Nothing worked, but he didn't seem to mind, perhaps resigned to their state of rot.

"*Nu*? Well? Where's the sun?" Abba looked up at a blanket of cloud. "I didn't come all this way to not get any heat," he said, closing his eyes. "And this wind, where did that come from? I detest wind."

"How can you hate wind?"

"It disturbs things."

I didn't even know where to start with that. Out of the corner of my eye, I saw Richard walking towards us. Dressed like a tennis player, he was wearing all-white; Adidas shorts, polo shirt, ankle-length socks and tennis shoes.

"Alright lads?" Richard asked, dropping his Aviator sunglasses onto his nose. "You having a good time?"

I nodded.

"So, what's the plan?"

"We might go for a drive or maybe a walk on a beach."

"Well if you fancy it later, we're doing kite-surfing and volleyball on the beach. And guess what? There'll be a free Thai massage for every member of the winning team. What do you think?"

"I'm not sure he's up to it."

34

"I realise that," he said, "but what about you?"

"I'll see."

"Suit yourself, but the free massage, aren't you tempted?" he said, nodding excitedly.

"Ah, excuse me," Abba said looking up at Richard. "Can you do something about the breakfast?"

"Pardon?" asked Richard.

"The breakfast. Any chance of some improvements?"

"What kind of improvements?" I asked.

"It's not exactly gourmet."

"You paid for it," I said.

"Yes I know that, but the least they can do is serve a decent cup of coffee, and this business of having to eat your breakfast by ten A.M.? I'm on holiday for God's sake."

Richard put his hands in his pockets and waited for us to stop.

"Anything specific you want?" Richard asked.

"Maybe a grapefruit, some oatmeal?" Abba asked and patted his stomach.

"Oatmeal? I don't know if we can get that fancy kind of stuff around here, but I'll talk to the chef, OK?"

"Thank you," I said.

"No bother. Let me know if you change your mind about the volleyball by the way, and we'll be doing shots and songs with the Irish Amigos from seven. I'll look into that oatmeal for you," he laughed as he walked away.

A couple of hours later, we drove through Playa de las Américas looking for the coast road out of town. Families laden with children and bags filled the beach, waiters stood outside restaurants waving menus at passers-by and half-naked party-goers left clubs, filling the air with bouncing bass.

"Any ideas of where to go?" I asked.

"Sure, how would I know? You're the man with the guidebook. Point towards the sun, and drive."

Finally on the coast road, I opened the window of the Cinquecento, accelerated and let the sultry air hug my body, feeling better now that we were moving.

"How are you getting on with *Herzog*?" Abba asked as we left Playa behind.

"I'm not sure yet. I've only read a bit."

"Bellow's another great. Like Roth. I adore Roth."

"You said that."

"But I do."

I moved into the fast lane, the road still steaming from an early morning shower.

"How's the therapy?" he asked.

"What?"

"What's she like?"

"Who?"

"Your therapist."

"How do you know it's a woman?"

"You told me."

"Did I?"

"You said you were seeing a Jewish woman," he said slowly.

I had no recollection of telling him about my shrink. Had he heard it from my mother?

"I think we're going to finish soon. That's the plan anyway. It's been going on a bit too long for my liking."

"How long?"

"A few months."

"Useful?"

"I suppose."

"Well, it's only worth doing if you find it useful. Otherwise what's the point?"

"I just don't seem to have much to say. I feel a bit," I paused, "foolish. She just stares at me the whole time."

"Foolish? Why would you feel foolish? If you've got something to say, then say it. Pull over, will you?"

I stopped on the hard shoulder. Abba got out of the car, and I watched him try to control his dribble of pee as the wind blew it onto a dusty cactus. The rush from the coffee had worn off, and my eyes itched. Feeling for Abba's pills, I took them out of my pocket and rolled them around my fingertips. They looked tempting, like sugary sweets. I had only agreed to come so I could have the chance to talk to him. Why was he doing all the talking? Why now? "Look at your questions. Make the first move." That's what my shrink said. I felt for the shape of my wallet in my back pocket and removed it. The piece of paper was still there.

"I can't get anywhere with mine," he said forlornly, settling himself back into the passenger seat.

"Your what?"

"Woman."

"You mean your therapist?"

"Yes, what's-her-name." Abba had a habit of using what's-their-name when he was too lazy to say someone's name, as if using someone's name might mean a closeness to that person, a friendship even. "Most of the time she stays *schtum*."

"And do you?"

"Do I what?"

"Talk."

"Well, I suppose it's *someone* to talk to. I don't know. Maybe I should also stop." He rolled down the passenger window. "We could stop at the same time. Compare notes. What do you think?" he laughed.

I ignored him.

"OK, be like that," he said. "It's here, it's here," he cried.

"What is?"

"The beach, the one I came to with your mother, turn right, now!" he said, gesturing.

Abba waved at the driver of a lorry as I swerved past it, and turned down a road signposted Playa La Arena.

Holding on to the top of the car door, Abba gingerly got out as the sun flickered through the clouds like a faint disc.

"This looks pleasant enough," he said outside the Café La Arena, an open-air restaurant on a promenade that overlooked a black sand beach, as if he'd planned it all along.

Pleasant. Another one of his favourite words. A word with little meaning. Agreeable. A word used when he didn't want to commit to really liking something, as if it would do because there were no better options, but frankly it could have been better all along and he was a bit disappointed by it all, and why couldn't it have been perfect just like he wanted? Like marvellous, I hated that word.

We waited to be served at a table that was set with a holder containing bottles of vinegar and olive oil, salt and pepper shakers and a bunch of folded paper napkins. Abba closed his eyes and rubbed his hernia before moving the ashtray to the next table, something he regularly did. I spent some time pressing a toothpick into my forefinger and thumb to see how long I could keep the pointy tips digging into my skin before they drew blood.

The sun emerged from behind the clouds as we ate *Papas Arrugadas*, rubbery calamari, a tomato and sweetcorn salad, and drank ice-cold beer. As I chewed a piece of squid, a small piece lodged in my throat. Coughing aggressively, I banged the table to get Abba's attention and after a mouthful of beer he looked up, rose languidly, walked around to my side of the table, and walloped me on my back knocking me forward, dislodging the squid. I recoiled and inhaled deeply, tears in my eyes.

After lunch, Abba held my wrist as we walked down a set of steps to the beach. We sat on the sand that stuck to our pale legs and arms. I went to dip my toes in the water, and watched children scream with delight as they bounced through the waves on floats. Abba lay down like a beached animal. I looked at him from the water's edge and hoped that finally, he was enjoying the heat he'd come for.

"What's the water like?" Abba asked as I sat down next to him.

"Warm, I might go for a swim."

"Think I'll sit in the shade," he said, licking his dry lips.

"I thought you liked the heat."

"I do, it's just making me a tad tired." Beads of sweat and melted sunscreen dripped from his shiny scalp.

"Nothing to do with the beer then?"

"Not at all."

"Is it helping your feet?"

"What? The beer?"

"No, the sun…"

"We've only been here for a day."

"So why are you tired?" I asked, exasperated.

"Must have been that bloody awful breakfast. Shall we make a move?" Abba looked to get up.

"Where to?"

"Let's drive up the coast. Take a look in the book and see if there's something interesting to see, will you?"

"Can't *you* have a look?"

"I thought you were the man who knows how to find places. You're the one that's been to China! Ohhhh, you used to get so upset when I didn't believe that you knew the right directions."

"No I didn't," I said, feeling like a child again.

Abba always dismissed my sense of direction when I was younger. I'd suggest one way, and he'd suggest another, never believing that I was right. Invariably I was. At which point he'd call me a "bloody know-all," and say that it was "pure luck" that I knew the right way. Tears would run down my red cheeks, but he'd be the one to sulk, like a toddler. Once home, my mother would persuade him to apologise. He'd give me a quick kiss, his breath stinking of whiskey.

"I think you'll find I was right, most of the time. You were the one who got upset," I said.

"Why did everyone think that I got upset?"

"Because you did."

"I wasn't upset. I disagreed. You all made such a big deal out of it. Every time, every time. Jesus. I just…"

"You just what?" I pressed him.

"Disagreed. Ahhh," he said, waving his hand at me, "forget it."

Pressing his wrists into the sand, Abba sat up, puffed out his cheeks and finished his beer. He tried to stand but collapsed back into a seated position, laughing to himself as he landed with a thud on his backside. Putting his hands in front of his body, he attempted to straighten his legs so he could curl up to stand, but fell forward onto all fours, his knees cracking the crusty sand. He gestured for help, so I put my arms around his chest and like a lifeguard pulling someone out of the water as he gripped my arms, I hoisted him up slowly, levering him upright.

I was very young when Abba sometimes gave me aeroplanes on my parents' bed at home. Lying on his back, pushing his feet into my ribs, he'd uncurl my hands slowly until our fingertips were just touching, and at the last moment he'd let go. My parents' bedroom seemed so vast as I'd fly high above him laughing, my arms and legs stretched out wide, unsteady, yet I was exhilarated by the feeling of weightlessness. After a few goes, I'd collapse onto his bed in a heap, the two of us rolling around, tickling and wrestling.

Our bodies were now in tandem as we stood up, his weight straining my hips, his breathing fast. Once fully upright he staggered forward a few steps until I stopped him from going any further.

"Thanks," he said, "I'll be in the car," and walked back across the sand.

I sat back down, finished my beer, and felt the gritty sand that had stuck to the bottom of the bottle. After a few minutes I checked to see if he'd got to the car. He was there, reclining in the passenger seat, his arm resting on the open window. During walks with him in Dun Laoghaire, Dublin, I often wondered why elderly couples would sit silently in their cars, rather than enjoy the fresh air. But he also liked to sit alone in the car, often waiting for my mother, sister and I to "get a move on."

One summer, when in primary school, our family was invited to a party at a friend's cottage outside Dublin. On arrival, I jumped out of the car and joined a game of tug of war. My team collapsed backwards like dominoes, the heavy rope stinging the palms of my hands.

After a while, I went in search of Abba. I was eager to show him a picture I'd drawn of the thatched cottage. He wasn't in the garden or the house. Gripping the picture, I approached our Fiat Ritmo that was parked on the side of the road, carefully avoiding the nettles and flowerbeds. I could see him through the windscreen, sitting in the driver's seat. His eyes were scrunched closed, as if he was forcing them shut, his lips gripped together, his forehead taut. I turned to look for my mother. Her eyes caught mine. She mouthed "leave him", but I continued to walk next to the side of the car while slowly running my finger along the scorching bonnet, removing a line of dust.

"Don't disturb him," my mother said, pulling me away from the car. As she did, I briefly looked at Abba, and for a split second noticed that he'd opened his tearful looking eyes and smiled at me.

No one at the party asked where Abba was. No one wanted to know if we were OK. As the bunting was being put away, a car door slammed, and he trundled towards us, hands in his pockets. Some of the men nodded and shook his hand as they stopped what they were doing. I saw my mother look over someone else's shoulder at him as she continued to nod mid-conversation, her lips sealed, a tender look in her eyes. He was passed a drink. His hand rested on my head as I wrapped myself tightly against his leg, gazing up at him, the picture still in my grasp.

I left my wallet, phone and sandals on the beach and waded into the sea fully clothed until I was almost submerged. The silver Star of David that hung from my necklace sparkled in the sunlight as it bobbed on the water. Bare-chested men sped past on jet skis, making waves that knocked me off balance. Inhaling deeply, I dunked under a wave, wondering how long I could hold my breath for. Salt water stung my eyes, so I closed them and started to count in the darkness that enveloped me. The sea groaned under water. Feeling empty, I curled my body into a foetal position and floated, waiting for someone to wrap their arms around me and pull me to the surface. I wanted to feel that tug, that grip, that force of someone else's skin against mine, the comfort of being rescued, exposed to air, my clothes dripping as I was flung up, and asked, are you OK? No-one came. Why would they? There was no lifeguard on the beach and Abba was still in the car. Just as my lungs started to tighten from a lack of air, I swam upwards, gasping as my mouth hit the surface, the sunlight stinging my eyes, seawater souring the back of my throat. Twenty-eight seconds. Not ready to go back to Abba just yet, I lay on the beach for a while and let the sun dry my clothes, leaving trails of crusty salt on my skin.

The guidebook recommended a visit to Masca, an ancient hillside village with an old church, local museum and vista. I thought a change of scenery into the mountains would be refreshing after the heat of the beach.

I drove slowly into aggressive clouds up a steep mountain pass, honking my horn as we navigated hairpin bends around the intestine-like track. Heavy raindrops banged onto the roof of the hollow car. Our breath misted the windows. I stopped twice so that Abba could pee.

After a few miles, we arrived in Masca, and parked next to a sandstone church in the middle of the town square. I ran on slippery cobbles to see if it was open, but it was locked.

Unsure of what to do, we found a café and huddled at a table next to a warm radiator against the rustic stone wall of the bar. I helped Abba steady his hand as he raised his cup of coffee to his lips. The only other customers were two men sitting in the opposite corner. Sodden waterproof jackets and trousers lay in a heap on the floor by their table. Speaking in what sounded like German, their voices boomed across the sparse room, masking the faint sound of Europop from a flashing jukebox.

Abba stared at the men over his glasses. He vigorously rubbed his hernia and twisted his signet ring around his little finger. I watched them wash down mouthfuls of fizzy beer and slap each other lightly on their backs. Every so often, one of them would catch my eye and laugh heartily.

Abba ordered a brandy that he cupped in his hand as he continued to glare at the men, swirling the alcohol faster and faster around the glass.

"That's it, they need to turn it down," he said, and scraped back his metal chair.

"Try to not let it bother you, we'll go in a minute."

"I can't. Eh, excuse me," Abba shouted across the bar.

"Jesus!"

"Can you turn the volume down a bit?" he said, patting his hand up and down.

"You can't tell other people to 'turn it down.'"

"Why not?"

"Come on, let's go."

"I'm not going until I finish my drink. What right do they have to disturb my peace?"

"It's a bar for God's sake," I sighed, "they can talk as loudly as they want."

The men ignored us, and Abba returned to his drink. After a few minutes, one of the men put down his beer heavily, stood up and walked towards our table, his boots squelching on the floor. I feared the worst. *Elderly Irish man and son get beaten up by two men in remote Tenerife village.* I was about to apologise for Abba's behaviour, when the man asked in a German accent, "do you have a car?"

"Yes," I said.

"Can you give us a lift please?"

"Where to?"

"Playa de las Americas. The weather isn't great you know."

"Where have you walked from?"

"The ocean. Three hours, all uphill. We missed the last bus. Gives us time to have a few beers." His belly wobbled as he chuckled.

"Where you staying?"

"The Hotel Optimist."

"No!" Abba cried, while staring at his drink.

Stunned, I turned to look at him.

"Excuse me one moment," I said to the man.

"Take your time," he said. He squeezed his ponytail that dripped onto the floor, and walked back to his table.

"What do you mean 'no'?" I asked.

"Listen, let me remind you, the war wasn't that long ago, they could be anyone. I don't want them in my car, I paid for that car."

"So? We can't leave them here, how are they going to get back to the hotel?"

"Why should I care? Anyway, they know."

"Know what?"

"That we're Jewish."

"Oh come on."

"Don't be so naïve. Does history mean nothing to you?"

"Of course it does."

"What would Roth make of this?"

"Who cares what Roth would think."

"I do!"

"Look, there are two men who are wet and need a lift. Don't be so bloody ridiculous."

"Doesn't it make you feel uncomfortable?"

"*Maspik*, enough," I insisted. "We're taking them."

Abba sniffed loudly and picked his nose.

I gave the man a thumbs-up.

"Just keep it down, OK?" Abba shouted across the bar.

We finished our drinks in silence. Abba now seemed more preoccupied with the legs of brandy on the inside of his glass than the men. I noticed a young woman working behind the bar. The curls of her long black hair and freckled face made me think of an ex-girlfriend, Aoife, and the time she met Abba at home in Dublin.

"We're going out," I shouted, as Aoife and I nearly fell down the stairs of our house, giggling.

"Here, can I meet your parents?" she asked.

I opened the door to the living room. Abba was sitting on our sofa, listening to what sounded like a Mendelssohn violin concerto.

"Jesus, is this all yours?" she asked, letting go of my hand and wandering in like an excited child. Aoife ran her fingers along shelves that heaved from the weight of Irish, Jewish and Israeli books and classical vinyl. She looked closely at a print by Chagall and ran her hand over the head of a sculpture of a seated naked pregnant woman carved from white stone.

Aoife had told me that her father, who was a policeman, wasn't best pleased that she was seeing a Jewish lad. She said that he planned to have "a quiet word with me" if we ever met. We couldn't keep our hands off each other though, snogging outside the International Pub, our lips and teeth clashing as we listened to repeats of *Jeremy* by Pearl Jam on our Walkmans.

"Quick drink?" Abba asked. I noticed a copy of *The Yellow Star*, a book of photographs about the Holocaust next to him.

"Have you read this?" Abba asked Aoife, holding up *The Yellow Star*.

I hadn't seen that book in ages. The cover had a black and white photograph of a young boy wearing shorts, a flat cap and a waist-length jacket with a yellow star that had been embroidered onto the chest pocket. His hands were held high, and he was surrounded by Gestapo who were pointing their guns at him. He looked terrified, alone, and so small as those around him watched on, helpless.

"Here, take a look," Abba said, passing Aoife the book.

"You don't have to," I said. "Come on, let's go."

Putting down her drink, Aoife sat back in the sofa and leant the book on her knees, catching strands of hair that fell onto her face and curling them behind her ears. She squirmed when she got to the photographs of bodies in liberated concentration camps piled on lorries, and shaved skeletal children with sunken eyes, staring into cameras through barbed wire. The violin concerto on the stereo intensified in the background, and the heat from the gas fire warmed my skin.

"Thanks," she said, handing me the book.

"Come on, have a proper look," Abba said.

"She did. Come on," I said.

"Go on, see what the bastards did. Kids, like you," Abba raised his voice.

"I think we'll…"

"What? You don't want to know?"

"Of course we do, it's just, we're meeting some friends."

"But Aoife hasn't, have you?"

"Abba, she just looked at it."

"One million children, that's how many they killed. Did you know that?" Abba took off his glasses and squeezed his eyes with his fingers. "There was a march on today," he continued, "somehow your mother convinced me to go. Said I should be there to support the bloody Intifada. I don't know what I was thinking. Well, I'm never doing that again. Some fella who was there was holding a protest sign of a Star of David with a Swastika in the middle of it. Can you believe it? On O'Connell Street, in front of the GPO, where I filmed *Insurrection*, comparing Israel to the Nazis?"

The bookshelves creaked as he went to pour another drink. "Your mother can go by herself next time."

"It's not her fault."

"It was nice to meet you," Aoife said.

"I hope they teach you some of this in school," Abba shook her hand.

"They do Abba, they do."

Kissing him on his forehead, I held his hand in mine for a moment. I stroked his bristly cheek. His eyes were moist with tears.

"You're a great man," he said, and held onto my neck. I loved it when he did that, the feeling of his warm hand on mine. His skin was always warm. I let him go, closed the door to the lounge and left him.

"Is he OK?" Aoife asked, taking my hand.

"He's fine. Come on, we're late." From the pavement, I could see that Abba had sat back down on the sofa, *The Yellow Star* in his hands.

Harold and Jürgen squashed into the back of the Cinquecento, their beer bellies rolling out of their t-shirts. The rain had cleared. A low glaze of sun rippled through the thinning clouds, ripening the day.

"UK?" Harold asked, as we drove back down the mountain pass towards the main road.

"No, Ireland," I said. "You guys from Germany?"

"Austria."

"You here on holiday?"

"Walking. The walking here is good. Tough, but fun. You?"

"Yeh, holiday. He likes to get some winter sun."

"He doesn't like loud sounds, eh?" Harold laughed as he edged forward between the seats.

"Sorry about that, he's, you know..."

"It's OK, old age, it's difficult."

"Is it?"

"My father was the same. The older he got the more he hated loud things. Pop music, car alarms. Smells. He had a real problem with strong smells, like when you blow out a match or cook eggs? He died last year. It was better for everybody. He was so angry by the end, shouting, screaming at everyone and everything. And he'd write these letters you know that just made no sense, as if it was the only way he could tell people what he really thought. And you know, I'm not even sure if he knew what he was angry about all the time," he laughed. "I don't think I ever really understood him. I think when you get old, like me and him soon," he said, slapping Jürgen on the knee. "You have less, you know, tolerance." It sounded like toleranzzzz. "Is that the right word?"

I nodded.

"Tolerance," he repeated, and slumped back into his seat.

Harold, Jürgen and Abba all snoozed as we wound back towards Playa de Las Américas, the word 'tolerance' spinning in my buzzing head like the italicised words of one of Herzog's unintelligible and long-winding letters that filled the first half of the book. He was writing at speed now. Letters of his dreams, his divorce, his concerns with foreign and homeland affairs, drugs, religion, socialism, everything tossing and turning through his frantic mind, as if he was under water wading to nowhere, flapping at something, but he had to keep going. He was unable to stop.

The shadows of palm trees grew longer as the lights of the hotels in Playa lit up the early evening sky. It was balmy and clear. We dropped Harold and Jürgen outside The Munich, a beer hall in the centre of town. They invited us in for a drink to say thank you. Abba looked tired and needed to eat, so I declined. As they took their jackets and rucksacks out of the boot, Abba peed behind the car, his shorts hanging by his ankles. I helped him pull them up, apologising to the bouncers who looked at us aghast.

"Glad we got rid of them," Abba said as we got back into the car.

"I liked them, you can learn a lot from other people you know."

"Well, you can never be too sure these days."

Entering the hotel lobby, I darted past Richard who was gathering players for the beach volleyball tournament. Abba and I sat on high stools at the bar, and Raul served us a couple of Jameson's and a bowl of nuts. No one seemed to mind as Abba lifted his t-shirt and injected a vial of Insulin into his abdomen. I drank quickly. The double shot made my head swim and released the tightness in my jaw and shoulders. A man in a black tuxedo sat at a white piano and started to play and sing Frank Sinatra's *I've Got You Under My Skin* to a smattering of applause. He wasn't bad, but it all felt a bit too jazzy and light. There was no bite to his beat, no strength in his voice, no power in his cadence. The words just drifted and evaporated into the low chatter of the bar as if he was doing it by rote rather than meaning. It was a song I knew well. I sang along to myself, gently tapping my glass to the rhythm. The chorus was coming up, but it wasn't loud enough. I took a mouthful of whiskey, turned on my stool to face the musician. *Give it some*, I thought. *Go on. Give it some.*

…Listen, it's after eleven and I still have to read plays by Mamet for a lecture at Trinity. I explained that I'd only done 'Glengarry Glen Ross' as you will remember, but they seem to regard me as some kind of damn expert, which I'm not, but I'd like to be. And yes, before I forget, I do have 'It all Adds Up' by Bellow, but I don't think I've read it. You should try reading some of the others, like 'The Dangling Man' and 'Herzog' which is one of my favourites of his. Did you know that my copy is signed by the great man himself? Pished he was one evening at a book signing in London, so I asked him to sign my copy that I'd brought especially. If you're lucky, I'll let you borrow it, but please be kind enough to send it back when you're done. Gaps in shelves don't look good. Mind you neither does a pished writer…

Insulin

The dizziness stopped when I opened my eyes. The LED alarm clock by my bed read 10:30. The apartment was still. I'd missed breakfast. I knocked lightly on Abba's bedroom door and edged it open. A flicker of sun lit his empty bed through gaps in the vertical blinds. His bed sheet was wrinkled, a pile of slept-on pillows sat in a heap, and a floral bedspread lay flung on the floor.

I coughed as I entered the steamy, windowless bathroom. An air vent whirred, and the overhead light dripped with condensation. Abba had displayed his medicines in a row on a shelf: Zocor, Aspirin, Valium, Naproxen, Warfarin, Heparin, Plavix, Prozac, Propranolol, Sertraline, Amitriptyline and Insulin, each bottle facing forward with instructions of how and when to take them. Globules of toothpaste had hardened on the ceramic basin, and spit stains had spattered the stainless steel taps. Using a towel, I meticulously cleaned the sink, wiped the mirror, washed away some stray hairs and swept the floor, leaving the bathroom pristine, like it was when we first arrived, as if I wanted to start our holiday again.

I separated the balcony doors releasing a hot breeze that warmed my goose-pimpled legs. My eyes squinted in the sunlight as I leant over the railings to see if Abba was sitting by the pool. Maybe he'd gone down for a coffee and to catch the sun. Nothing, apart from Harold and Jürgen and a few eager swimmers doing laps.

"Abba?" I cried half-heartedly for some reason from our third-floor balcony. A low-flying plane cut through the clouds.

"Excuse me," I called and waved at a man holding the hand of a young boy wearing armbands as they walked towards the kids' pool close to our block.

He ignored me.

"Excuse me," I shouted.

He looked up, blocking his eyes from the glare of the sun that bounced off the whitewashed walls of the hotel.

"You haven't seen an old, bald man by any chance, have you?"

"What?" the man asked.

"An old man with glasses. Have you seen him? He's probably wearing a grey t-shirt or something. You haven't seen him, have you?"

The man shook his head, grabbed the boy's arm and quickened his pace.

"Daddy, why is that man only wearing his pants?" I heard the boy ask as I went back inside, stubbing my little toe on a table leg.

"Fuck," I snapped.

The skin of my bare legs stuck to the pleather sofa as I sat down. I closed my eyes. My head spun viciously. I opened my eyes hoping Abba would just appear. He was lost, I knew it. I began to rehearse excuses for losing him. What would I tell my mother? He's old enough to look after himself. I can't be with him every minute of the day. I have my own life to lead. Why am I even here? We'd had a few drinks in the bar the night before listening to some jazz, but we'd had an early night... well, early-ish. We

55

hadn't argued. I thought we were getting on quite well actually, even though we'd managed to disagree about Israel at some point during dinner, and then he told me that he'd wished he'd stayed there or something, and I told him he was being ridiculous, but overall, it was a good evening. The fish we had was good. Yes, he drank a fair bit, but isn't that the norm? He'll turn up at some stage. He always does.

In an effort to wake up, I threw some cold water on my face in the kitchen and downed a couple of paracetamol, drinking straight from the tap. Maybe he went for a walk on the beach. That was it. He'd gone. Alone.

A few years before, when I was still living at home in Dublin, I dropped Abba off on the edge of Sandymount Strand for a walk. He knew the expansive beach well. Walkable at low tide, it connects part of the south side of Dublin Bay, from Poolbeg to Dun Laoghaire. I often went with him. Leaving the thrum of the traffic behind, we'd walk until we reached an isolated sandbank way out in the bay then stop to watch the lighthouse beacon turn before heading back to shore.

"See you back here in an hour," I said as I left him. I watched Abba walk off, his shoes leaving imprints on the waterlogged sand. He'd tucked a scarf into his coat, and his digital camera hung from his neck. It was a clear late-autumnal afternoon, the perfect time to capture the sunset. The sky was filled with pinks, reds and yellows, flooding puddles of seawater and sand that rippled out to sea for miles.

An hour later, I pulled up in the car park as a dark blueness enveloped the bay. Dogs jumped into car boots as I listened to the six o'clock news on the radio. I stood by the car and smoked a cigarette while looking into the distance. Perhaps he'd got his bearings wrong and walked towards the lighthouse, I thought, in which case he'd return on the promenade along the shore. I checked my mobile phone. He hadn't called. Then again, he rarely turned on his phone. "Sure, why would anyone want to talk to me?" he'd ask.

I turned off the car radio, walked down to the shore and back. Nothing. Fuck it. I ran quickly along the promenade, lengthening my stride, my keys jangling in my coat. After what seemed like five minutes, I bent over to relieve a stitch, my breathing laboured and wheezy, then continued to see if he'd gone as far as the Martello Tower. He was nowhere to be seen.

Twenty minutes later I jogged back to the car park, expecting to see him standing by the car. Through a thicket of trees ahead of me, I noticed some blue lights bouncing in the darkness, heard the faint crackle of a walkie-talkie and a whirring of blades overhead. I approached the car slowly. My heart missed a beat. The traffic paused. The wind slowed. I knew I could move but didn't. I knew I could cry out but didn't. I knew I could see but didn't want to look. My thoughts hung like a lighthouse beacon unable to turn full circle. I stood, almost floating, as two coastguards brushed past me and ran to rescue a man who was stumbling towards the shore. It was Abba.

"Sure they didn't need the helicopter. All this fuss. It was nothing," Abba said, recounting the story from his hospital bed later that evening, his only injury some freezing feet. "And did I tell you?" he laughed, "the person who saw me waving my scarf knows your mother. Can you believe it? You should have seen

57

the light, it was delicious."

"Didn't you see the tide come in?" I asked.

"Nope, but I think it saw me."

"It's not funny, for God's sake. What were you thinking? You know when the tide comes in. How many times have we done that walk? I couldn't see you."

"I got some great shots. I'll go to the printers tomorrow and get you a copy."

"I don't want a bloody print."

"I didn't mean to frighten you."

"Well you did a good job trying!" I said angrily, "and Imma's really bloody upset you know."

"Tell her I'll be fine by the time she comes home."

I shook my head.

"Lis-ten," he accentuated the 't' as if emphasising a point. He sat up. "Any chance you could pop out and get me a decent meal. The food here is bloody awful."

"What?"

"Last time I was here, your mother brought me a wonderful steak and some salad. Made the whole stay worthwhile."

"Where am I going to get a steak at this hour?"

"How would I know?"

"Look, you'll be lucky if I can find you a bloody sandwich." I sighed, walked out of the hospital ward and left him scrolling through the photos on his camera, an electric blanket wrapped around his feet.

This was typical Abba. The drama of what happened was the important bit. It gave him a story to recount, a story of survival, how he'd endured but still came out alive, and with the photos.

What a hero. But it annoyed me that he could see the funny side of an event in which he could have died, and I couldn't.

I grabbed a croissant from the breakfast buffet and ran to the pool to check if Abba had turned up. There he was, the back of his head poking over the top of a sun lounger, under the shadow of a palm tree. Piz Buin sunscreen, his sun hat, and a drained coffee cup sat on a table next to him. The tension in my head eased. I looked up to our balcony. How had I not seen him?

"Abba," I said, tapping his shoulder. He didn't stir. His glasses hung from a cord against his chest. His face and neck were unshaven, and he was wearing his red swimming trunks. Roth's *Everyman* lay open, face down, covering his hernia.

"Ah, you're up," he said, opening his eyes.

"Where have you been?"

"Here."

"Since when?"

"Well, I had some breakfast, and came to read in the sun. It's marvellous to finally get some heat. Let's stay here today."

"I thought you'd gone somewhere or something. Would you mind telling me before you plan to just go off next time?"

"I looked in on you, but you were sleeping so deeply. Ohhhhh, I used to love watching you sleep. Such a beautiful little boy, with that thick head of hair of yours."

I rolled my eyes.

"What time did you wake up?" I asked.

"Early. These bloody feet are like an alarm clock," he said, closing his eyes and directing his face towards the sun.

*

I dragged a chair next to Abba and sat down. A smell of coconut drifted through the hot air as women massaged sunscreen and oils into their skin. Two men spent a few minutes egging each other on to dive into the pool from the five-metre diving board. Eventually one of them jumped, landing spread-eagled in the water.

Abba squirted some Piz Buin onto his head but couldn't reach his back, so I squeezed some cream into the palm of my hand and worked it into his spine and around his broad shoulders. His skin was warm and supple. As a child, I sometimes offered to give him 'Maestro's Special Massage' in exchange for ten pence. I'd sit him down in an armchair, put on his favourite Mozart Horn concerto, and suggest that he closed his eyes. I'd dig my thumbs into his back, pinching and quickly tapping his shoulders before massaging his head. He'd flinch, his shoulders rising to his ears. I'd push harder, prodding my fingers deeper into his tight, sinewy muscles, embedding my nails into his skin, unsure of what I was doing, and why, but hoping it was relaxing him. "OK, that's enough," he'd say after a few minutes, stopping my hands with his to say that I was stronger than I looked.

I unfolded the piece of paper with my questions after removing it from my wallet, then held it inside *Herzog*. We had six days left. I knew I had to start somewhere. Abba would be relaxed after a day in the sun, so I thought I could ask question one that evening, over dinner.

"Hi."

It was Richard, standing silhouetted against the sun.

I closed *Herzog*.

"What're you reading'?" he asked, without looking up from his Sony Ericsson flip phone.

"*Herzog*, by Saul Bellow." The heat stuck to my forehead like a piece of duct tape.

"Who?"

"Saul Bell-ow," I said loudly.

I turned my head and caught the eye of an elderly woman in a wide-brimmed hat. She peered at me over a Bible she was reading that looked similar to the one I'd seen on a shelf in our apartment.

"I heard you the first time. Any good?"

"He recommended it," I said, nodding at Abba.

"What's it about?" He pulled up a chair alongside me.

Couldn't he just leave me alone? Why did he care so much? There were plenty of other people he could bother, like the girls painting their toenails over the crinkly pages of a fashion magazine, or the lads diving. But he seemed intrigued by Abba and me, as if we had gate-crashed his party.

"It's about this Jewish guy, Moses…"

"Nice name," Richard laughed.

"He lives in New York and has broken up with his second wife. He's going a bit mad, I don't know, insane, and he doesn't have any friends or anyone to talk to, and just seems to hate everything and everyone, so ends up writing letters to his family members and friends that he doesn't see anymore, and politicians and mayors and teachers and anyone he can think of. Can you imagine spending your whole life writing your thoughts and crazy ideas in letters and notes? That's what he does. He becomes obsessed with writing letters, as if it's the only way he can get revenge on his wife who has left him and on everyone else who he thinks has done him wrong in some way or another. And he hates everything, especially modern or new things, it's so weird. There's a car crash at some point, but I haven't got to that bit yet." My eyes began to water from the glare of the sun.

"I like writing letters," Richard said. "Not like that mind you, but I write to my dad when I can. We're close. He likes getting them. Well, that's what he says. He says that he can't work out that email thing. He's funny that way. Hasn't turned on a mobile phone in his life. Not sure he'd know what to do with it. Can you believe it?"

"Ah," Abba said, looking up from Roth, "any chance of a drink?"

"I'm not the bar man," Richard laughed. "Did you get your oatmeal by the way? I left it out with your name next to it."

"No."

"That's strange. Maybe someone else took it. I'll make sure it gets left out for you again tomorrow."

"But I did find half a grapefruit. Too damn sweet. You can't get the sour ones at home these days anymore. You know what they do with them? They bring them all the way from South America and freeze them. Why on earth would they want to freeze a grapefruit?"

"Hello!"

I looked up. It was Harold. I waved back.

"Listen, if you want my advice," Richard said, "there's a shop down the road that sells all the bestsellers, that's if you want something a bit lighter. You are on holiday you know." He smiled knowingly as he stood up.

"It's too bloody hot. I'm going for a swim," Abba said.

Abba held my hand as he carefully eased himself onto the ladder of the swimming pool and stepped down into the water. I watched him push away on his back, and propel his arms over his head a few times, but after a few strokes he bumped into a woman lying on a lilo. She yelped as he splashed chlorinated water onto her bronzed body. Abba ignored her, stood up, spat out some pool water, and turned to float on his back, his wet chest hair sparkling in the sun.

"I'm a bit peckish. See what they have for lunch will you," he said as I helped him up the ladder a few minutes later, "just have to pop upstairs."

Holding my shoulder to steady himself, Abba slid into his flip-flops which slapped against the paving stones as he headed back inside the hotel, his togs leaving a trail of water behind him. I sat back down, re-opened *Herzog* and willed myself to learn some of my questions off by heart, but when I tried to recount what I'd written I couldn't seem to remember them, as if they were being erased from my mind as quickly as they went in. I tried one last time to learn them without looking at the piece of paper, but as I did, a drop of sweat fell from my forehead onto my handwriting, smudging the ink.

The air-conditioned apartment was a relief from the midday sun. I noticed that Abba had changed into his chinos and short-sleeved shirt and was sitting with his legs crossed on the sofa, his arms resting on his lap.

"Going somewhere?" I asked.

"How many more days are we here?"

"Six."

"I knew we didn't bring enough."

"Enough what?"

"Insulin."

"What?"

"I need twelve more. I just took the last one."

"Where's the rest of them?"

"How should I know?"

"Did you count them?"

"Check if you like."

"Tell me you counted them before we packed."

"Your mother counted them."

"Why didn't you do it?"

"She offered."

"Could they be anywhere else?"

"Like where?"

"Did you look in the bathroom?"

"That's all we brought."

"How could *you* not bring the right amount of Insulin?"

"Why are you getting so angry?"

"How long till you need another one?"

"A few hours."

"So what do we do?"

"Find a doc. Quick."

Recommended by Richard, the Red Cross Clinic was in a single-storey building across the road from The Munich. A crowd of drinkers was filling the pavement outside the bar, soaking up the lunchtime sun.

"Must be a decent doc with a name like Steinberg," Abba said, pointing to a sign on the entrance. He knocked on the glass sliding doors as we waited outside. They edged open, so he pulled them apart and marched towards the reception desk. Before he got there, he paused to look at a framed poster on the wall of a sunny beach with an empty deck chair under the shade of a sun umbrella. A book lay face down in the sand next to the deck chair, and a glass of white wine sat on a wooden table. Across the top it read, "just what you've been waiting for". Abba stared at the poster for a few moments, his attention taken by the picture in front of him before he gathered himself and continued to the reception desk.

Barely visible behind the counter was an elderly woman talking in Spanish on a cordless telephone. Labels were stuck to the sides of the monitor and her face, lit by the screen, was thick with foundation. A pair of tortoiseshell glasses perched on the tip of her nose.

"Excuse me," I said.

She gestured to a row of chairs lined up against a wall in an adjacent waiting room.

"Excuse me," I coughed. She flicked her hand at me.

"I need to see Doctor Steinberg, please," Abba butted in.

Placing the telephone on her shoulder, she glared at us over her glasses.

"Yes?" she asked.

"My father needs to see a doctor," I said.

"What's the problem?"

"He's diabetic and needs more Insulin."

"OK. Doctor Steinberg will see you."

"How long is the wait?"

"Fifteen minutes, *más o menos*, more or less."

As we waited the room filled with the sound of a baby crying and an elderly man who tapped his cowboy boots on the tiled floor. I rubbed my skin to stay warm and deleted a couple of text messages from Orange about cheap European calls. Abba dozed in between trips to the toilet and stood up every time the receptionist called a patient's name.

"Can't he get a bloody move on?" Abba sighed after half an hour, "I'm missing the hottest part of the day."

There was nothing else to do. My questions flickered in and out of my mind as I tried to recite them in my head. I had to get him talking. Use a memory. That's what my shrink said.

"Abba," I said hesitantly.

"What can I do for you?"

"Do you, ehhh, remember?"

"What?"

"Do you remember when we went to the Aran Islands, just you and me, over a New Year's weekend?"

"Did we?"

"Around ten years ago."

"Really? I don't remember," he coughed loudly. "I'm parched, can you get me a glass of water?"

"Mister Lentin?" the receptionist bellowed.

"Finally."

"Abba."

"What now?"

I handed him a crumpled plastic wallet with his medical documents, passport, travel insurance and list of prescriptions then slouched back into a chair. The receptionist banged at a keyboard like a heavy hammer, and every so often the crackle of a Dot Matrix printer pierced the room. At some point, the cacophony of electronics stopped, and the receptionist appeared with a bucket of steaming liquid and a mop which she sloshed across the floor. I stood up. My legs were restless. My hands were clammy. I had to get out. An acrid smell of bleach lodged in my throat. I made an effort to concentrate, trying to think of the sentences on the piece of paper, redoubling the efforts in my mind, trying to make them relevant, but they soon scattered and were lost. I began to wonder if all of this was a mistake, and even if I did start talking and manage to explain to Abba what I wanted to know that nothing would come out, and instead I would be the one apologising for upsetting him.

Half an hour later, Abba returned to the waiting room followed by Doctor Steinberg who was wearing a lab coat with the sleeves rolled up above his elbows. He had the look of a successful uncle.

"Your father was telling me that you are chaperoning him on holiday. That's very good of you," said Steinberg, who spoke with a South African accent.

He smiled at me.

"Well, if that's everything," Steinberg said, "see Maria on your way out. Come back whenever you need to."

"Oh, I will," said Abba, "and thanks for the restaurant tip. What's it called again?"

"La Torre del Mar, in La Caleta."

"By the way, have you read any Roth?"

"Who?"

"Roth, you know Philip Roth, the writer?"

"Never heard of him."

"What's the one I'm reading?" he asked, turning to me.

"*Everyman*," I said.

"That's it. It's really very funny. This poor old fella has this wrong with him and that wrong with him, he's marvellous."

"That's very kind," Steinberg interrupted, "I have some patients waiting."

"Come on, let's go," I said, holding Abba's elbow.

"He's Jewish, you know," Abba continued.

"Who is?" Steinberg asked.

"Roth, of course."

"That's great, but I'm not Jewish."

"No, no, of course not, I just thought—" The squeal of the Dot Matrix printer burst the room. Abba rubbed his hernia.

"Well, enjoy the rest of your holiday."

They shook hands.

Abba stopped in front of the automatic doors as we moved to leave the surgery.

"*Nu*! Well!" Abba gesticulated at the doors.

"Did you get what you needed?" I asked.

"Can't she open the bloody doors?"

"Did you get it?"

"Get what?" he snapped.

"The prescription," I said.

"For the life of me I thought he was… He told me he knows people who've just been to Israel on holiday."

"Well?"

"What?"

"The Insulin prescription, did you get it?"

"Oh that, yes," he said as the doors separated open.

The dry afternoon heat hit me like a sharp desert wind, the sun low and raw. It looked like the street had been blown dry. The crowd was now thick outside The Munich, and two men were sitting on the bonnet of the Cinquecento necking bottles of beer.

"Eh, do you mind?" Abba hollered at the men. The men didn't move. "Look, can you get off my car. Bloody yobbos," he muttered.

"What did you say?" One of the men turned his head. I noticed a stud earring in his ear that sparkled in the sun. His face was red, his neck burnt.

"Get in the car," I said to Abba. "He didn't say anything," I said, turning to the men.

"I asked you to get off my car."

"Leave it, come on."

The man with the earring jumped down from the bonnet, and, still gripping his bottle of beer, opened his arms confrontationally. "There. I am off your fucking car," he said, kicking one of the front tyres, and stared at Abba for a few seconds, mouth open, head bent to one side, not moving. I fumbled for the key but dropped it as I tried to open the car door. The dizziness returned as I stood up. The other man slid off the bonnet. I froze, fear clutching my breath as he wrapped his hairy arm that was matted with sweat around my shoulders.

"Get your hands off him," Abba cried, waving his shaking hand.

"Relax, I'm only joking with you," he said, giving me a firm squeeze, his nails digging into my shoulder. Stretching his arm around the front of my head he took a swig of beer. His breath was stale. He held me close for a few seconds. It felt like hours, the sun burning the top of my head. Eventually he let me go and gave me a shove. The man laughed. I wanted to thank him, say cheers or offer to buy him a drink or something, but my legs almost buckled under me. I got in the driver's side and slammed the car door. I helped Abba fasten his seat belt. I was eager to get away from the area, from the doctor's surgery, from The Munich. I'd had enough drama for one day.

A smattering of French and German greeted us as we entered La Torre del Mar restaurant in the fishing village of La Caleta later that evening. The sound of fryers sizzling and the smell of a charcoal grill wafted towards us from behind a glass counter. Waiters shouted orders through a hatch into the kitchen, and delivered plates spread along their arms.

Sitting outside, I ripped open a packet of crunchy bread sticks. Abba sprinkled the crumbs that had fallen onto the table with salt and whispered, "*ha-motzi lechem min ha-aretz*", the prayer for breaking bread, even though it wasn't *Shabbat* and said "Amen". He winked at me. We pressed our fingers into the grit and licked them.

"*Sí*," a waiter said, arriving at our table. "*Mesa cinco*, Rafael!" he shouted at the kitchen. "*Mesa cinco!*"

"What's the fish of the day?" Abba asked.

"Cherne, and if you'd like seafood, we have *Gambas a la plancha*. The special is Tenerife fish stew. Marco, *botella de agua, a la siete, vamos!*"

"I'll try the stew," Abba said.

"To drink?"

"Jameson's?" Abba looked up eagerly at the waiter.

"And a bottle of white wine please," I said. "Maybe Steinberg was right, this place doesn't look too bad."

"Sure I've been trying to tell you that for years."

"Tell me what?"

"That docs are always right," Abba said, his glass of whiskey shaking in his hand. "Do you have a good GP?" he asked. And then the lecture began about why I needed to have a regular GP, and why did I always rely on the receptionist in the surgery to find me a doctor who was free, and couldn't I find a doctor at a small surgery, some place where I could see the same person whenever I needed, someone I could trust and talk to, just like he did? All this codology about computers and seeing a different doctor every time wasn't good for anyone, and what did a computer know anyway and if he'd relied on computers, he'd be dead long ago and wasn't Steinberg a great find, just marvellous?

"If you still lived at home and you needed to see a doc, I'd take you to one of mine," he said.

"Oh please, your cocktail of drugs hasn't exactly worked, has it?"

"Look, when you get to my age, you need a little something to keep you going. Don't knock what you don't know."

"I can do without people prescribing me things I don't need."

"Wait and see my son, wait and see…"

"*Señor*, your fish," the waiter said, "and, Tenerife stew *señor*."

"Ahhh," Abba said knocking back the remainder of his whiskey. "So, what's your cholesterol?"

"Can't we just eat?" I asked as I poured the wine.

Abba tucked a napkin into his shirt. We ate and drank, almost in tandem.

"Any good?" he asked.

"Not bad," I said, picking a sticky bone out of the side of my mouth. "Yours?"

"I think it's been frozen." He paused. "Damn, I forgot to take the Insulin. I'll be back in a minute."

I held the fish head, tore the central bone from the flesh and let it dangle in front of my eyes. The tail was charred and the bones, some thick like nails, some thin like pins, hung perfectly formed. As I dropped the fish skeleton onto a spare plate, I heard a thump, as if a sack of cement had been dropped onto the ground.

"*Señor!*" I heard a man shout, followed by a faint scream. The music stopped. I scraped back my chair, stood up and threw my napkin onto the table.

"Jesus," I said, as I saw two waiters lift Abba up from his knees by the entrance to the bathroom. He'd slung his arms over their shoulders and was hobbling, wearing only one flip-flop. I pulled up his trousers that had come loose at the waist, and replaced one of the waiters to take on Abba's weight. The restaurant fell silent apart from a few diners who whispered to each other, and looked on as we walked back to our table. Gingerly, Abba sat down.

The waiter slammed down a whiskey. "Is he OK?"

I nodded and placed my hands over Abba's as he drank.

"Who the bloody hell puts a step just outside the bathroom?" he asked.

"Have you hurt anything?"

"I'll know in the morning," he said, rubbing his wrists and

72

the side of his forehead.

"Another?" I asked.

He shook his head. His cheeks were flushed, and his eyes had a resigned expression. The music started up again as we continued to pick at our food, Abba pausing to take two pills.

"You look tired, let's get you home," I said.

The waiter left a saucer on the table with the bill and two mints. "*Helado para los niños,* Marco," he shouted as he walked away.

"Shall we go?" I asked.

"*Yalla,* come on."

I knocked back the remainder of my wine and helped Abba up. The waiter shook the tablecloth, tossing what was left of our crumbs onto the floor.

I rested my back against the sloping wall on the balcony of our apartment. I lifted my head to the clear, dark sky, and dangled one leg over the side. I reckoned the drop was five, maybe six metres. Far enough to break a few bones but not do any real damage. The ash from my cigarette flew into the breeze, and I counted just how many more days I'd have to do this. I heard the air vent of the bathroom spin and the toilet flush.

Lying in bed later, the dizziness had disappeared, but I found it hard to close my eyes. Every time I turned my head, the tender muscles in my neck twinged from the grip of the drinker outside Doctor Steinberg's surgery. I could hear everything: a fly crashing into a light bulb in the hallway, bottles being poured into a bin, the beeps of hotel doors being opened. I thought of Abba sleeping in a foetal position, gripping his sheet tightly up to his chin, his head propped on his pillows, his feet poking out from the other end of the bed. Sneaking into the bathroom I lifted two sachets of Solpadeine from Abba's medicine kit, tore the foil lining and dropped the tablets into a wet glass. Immediately, their powdery effervescence bubbled and dissolved. I untwisted the bottle of Jameson's and poured.

…And what's all this about feeling sad because girlfriend number one went home early? Listen to me bucko, there'll be no such thoughts while the British government, or is it the Scottish, or whoever the hell it is, is paying for your education at my expense! Out damn spot, out, or I'll send you a personal complaint letter, and you know what that means. As a penance for even entertaining such thoughts, I shall set you some handwriting homework! Next time, consult the sages before taking any action… or better still, call me for advice…

Wine Tasting

Torrents of rain and bursts of wind battered the window of my bedroom. I pressed my nose against the glass and watched cars and airport coaches drive across flooded potholes that dotted the car park. A group of men loitered outside Gerry's Bar that advertised 'all you can eat full English breakfasts for twelve euros' on a flashing neon sign. They huddled under a torn awning that flapped like a sail in the wind, wearing t-shirts with 'The Great Escape' emblazoned on the back, flip-flops and jeans that stuck to their drenched legs. With little else to do, I watched them josh with each other as they dragged on cigarettes cupped in their hands, and sipped pints, wondering why Abba and I couldn't be like that with each other.

The warmth of the duvet caressed my body as I fell back onto my bed. I listened to what sounded like a television next door, faint high-pitched notes of a scale being played up and down piercing the thin walls. A chase was on. "I'll get you next time," a shrill voice cried. The music built to a crescendo of plucked violins, vibrating horns, squeals, shrieks and ya-hooos, before a terrifying screech of brakes. A pause. And then the cracking and breaking of timber crashing and debris flying through the air. Boom. Another pause. Beep-beep. "I'll get you next time." A child giggled hysterically. "Turn it down!" an adult voice shouted.

I laughed, my head still zippy from Abba's 'Solps on the beach' cocktail from the night before.

I wondered if I should suggest to Abba that we go to Gerry's for breakfast. All the foods he hated: bacon, pork sausages, fried eggs, black pudding, hash browns, baked beans, ketchup, brown sauce, milky tea. He had no problem buying pork salami when I was young, but he couldn't stomach bacon. While my friends walked to synagogue every Saturday morning in their suits, he'd take me to buy his illicit treat of salami from McGill's Deli in Dublin. We'd return home with slivers of the greasy sausage, wrapped in greaseproof paper, encrusted with cracked black pepper, and usually a block of soft Gubbeen cheese that he'd leave sitting unwrapped on the counter so that it could breathe as otherwise the cold would kill the flavour, and what's the point in eating cold cheese, he'd say.

Rain spattered my feet as I sat on the balcony in shorts and a t-shirt and finished a cigarette. The air was tight. The lifeguard I'd seen the day before busily stacked sun loungers and emptied ashtrays by the pool, draining them of filthy water into a bucket. *Herzog* lay face down on the balcony, the pages sodden and matted together.

"Meh," Abba said, standing behind me at the balcony door. He was naked apart from his vest that just about reached his waist.

"How's the head?" I asked.

"It's nothing…"

Abba looked like he'd shrunk in the night. A bruise like a blotchy cloud of blue ink had appeared on the side of his forehead. It darkened to purple as I touched it. He flinched and shook my hand away.

77

Poking his head forward, he looked to the thick grey sky and grimaced. His hernia hung from his abdomen. His buttocks was flat and pale, and stretch marks glistened like snail trails down the inside of his thighs.

"Maybe put some clothes on?" I suggested.

"What's the forecast?"

"This isn't a nudist colony you know."

"Oh, now, that would be nice. Better than this place. I've nothing to hide," he said. "I think the Germans have it right with all their nudity. Maybe I'll sunbathe naked today. That's if the bloody sun comes out. Anyway, what's there to be ashamed of? I can't change my body, not now at least. It's not as if anyone's going to find me, you know, sexy. Your mother certainly doesn't. Let me ask you, do I embarrass you?"

"Are you going to get dressed?"

"Have a look for something to do. I'm going to shave."

I took *Herzog* inside and pressed a tea towel onto it, as if I was blotting the words from the page.

I stood in the doorway to the bathroom and watched Abba lather his face. Condensation covered the mirror as steam rose from the sink. His razor shook in his hand as it bounced on his skin, removing patches of shaving cream, leaving a few specks of blood behind. Moving towards him, I gently uncurled his fingers from the razor, and took it from him. With the forefinger and thumb of my other hand, I pinched and stretched his skin taut, loosening the tension and gently opening the pores just like he'd taught me.

I stood behind Abba as I worked, his hand holding mine, my

belly pushing against his back. Keeping my fingers on his skin, I ran the blade against the coarse hairs on his cheeks and chin, slicing through the cream methodically, gradually exposing his features. His cheeks were heavy and sagging as if he was carrying something in them. His nose was straight, bulbous at the tip, his lips full.

After every glide of the razor, I knocked it against the inside of the sink releasing the residue of the cream and sliced hair that floated in the water. Pursing his mouth closed, I shaved under his nose, careful not to catch the blade on his lips, then hovered it over his head and around his ears to trim any stray hairs. The thickness of the emollient filled my nostrils.

I was six when I sliced open my cheeks while shaving. I don't know why I did it. Abba found me standing silently in the bathroom, blood dripping onto the floor from my face. I gripped the worn wooden handle of his razor, unable to let it go. I didn't cry. He removed the razor, pressed his warm hands on my cheek, and buried me into his chest.

As I finished shaving him, he closed his eyes. I proceeded to massage the leftover cream into his cheeks, pressing my thumbs against the shaving nicks and circling my fingers first around his eyes, then under his nostrils, followed by his jaw and across the front and back of his neck. At that moment I didn't want to let go of his clean, smooth skin in my rough hands.

"Look, it's not my fault the weather's rubbish, is it?" Richard said, sitting behind a desk in the lobby of the hotel. He was wearing a short-sleeved shirt and a thin tie with the words 'Sun-Seeker Holidays' woven diagonally in yellow thread on the front.

79

"I only asked if you knew how much longer it was going to be like this," I said.

"I'm not a weatherman you know. This is way beyond what I get paid to do," he said, leafing through a folder of brochures. "Let's see. There's the Crocodile Farm, but it's outside, so they're probably closed. Folk art museum? You seem the kind that would like that kind of thing."

I sighed.

"Cigar making factory? You smoke, don't you? Car museum? I've not been there myself, but I hear it has some buses and trams. Might be interesting, and it's near a beach. Mind you, that's not going to be much help today, is it?"

I tapped my feet.

"Cookery classes? The aquarium?" He raised his head. "What about wine? Your dad likes a drink, doesn't he? Wine tasting, there you go. I knew it was here somewhere. Bodega Ruiz," he said, slamming down a leaflet.

"Where's that?"

"On the road to the volcano. Last time I was there I took a hen party with me and, ehh, let's just say, that didn't end well. Mister Ruiz hasn't spoken to me since. Tell him I say hi. He might give you a discount."

I grabbed the leaflet.

"Oh, you're welcome," Richard shouted after me.

Mud spattered the back of my legs as I bolted across the car park through driving rain and into a café next door to Gerry's Bar. I ordered a double espresso. It tasted of cigar smoke. Standing at the counter by the window, I watched tanned holidaymakers drag their suitcases and children across the car park and onto buses, off to catch a damp flight home. I dipped a sugar cube into the coffee, and watched the liquid rise up through it like a magnetic force, colouring it grain by grain. Stirring the coffee with a teaspoon, I studied the spirally swirl of the froth and sipped. I flicked through the contents of my wallet, tempted to look at my questions again. My mind drifted, as it often does when I'm travelling on a train. Sometimes I'd ride the underground to the last station on the line, and start my journey again, preferring the comfort and warmth of the rocking motion, careering anonymously through the city, headphones on, not speaking, just letting the movement caress my mind, warm my skin. When I was underground, I didn't have to make an effort, I could just be; the effort of having to drag myself off the carriage seemed too difficult.

I flicked the leaflet across the breakfast table. "Wine tasting," I said.

"*Be-emet*? Really?" Abba asked, looking at the pictures. "This place isn't known for its wine. It's a volcanic island."

"You seemed to enjoy what we had last night."

"If you say so… Where is it?"

"Somewhere near the volcano."

"Ah, volcanic wine, even better."

"I'm quite happy to stay here and read if you'd like?"

"It's your holiday as well," he said, his mouth full of oatmeal.

"I thought you wanted to do something."

"I'm easy."

What does that even mean? I thought.

"If you want to go, let's go," he said.

"Well, it sounds better than the folk art museum."

"Sounds interesting."

I finished some cold scrambled eggs that tasted of cardboard and Abba sliced into his grapefruit and removed the flesh with a spoon, squirting juice across the table and onto my glasses.

"Abba? I'd like to, you know..." I coughed. "Talk a bit, while we're here," I blurted out, surprising myself.

"Is this about the trip to Aran?"

"Oh that, no. I mean, there's some other stuff I've been meaning to talk to you about."

"You can talk to me about anything, you know that. Anything specific?"

"This, us, you know, you and me."

"What about you and me?"

An elderly woman with blue eye shadow nodded at me as she sat down at the next table. There was something I recognised about her, and then realised it was the same woman I'd seen reading the bible by the pool the day before.

"Maybe later," I said.

"Why not now?"

"It's not exactly the right place, is it?" I whispered, looking over at the woman.

"Why are you whispering?"

"Later, OK?"

"Is this about your mother and me?"

"No... yes... not really." I hesitated. "I don't know. It's more about me, than you."

"Well, whenever you're ready." Abba rubbed the back of his neck. "Where's that draft coming from?" he asked, looking at the door to the pool that had been left ajar. "Will someone close that bloody door?" he shouted. No one responded.

Two hours later, we bounced in the Cinquecento along a rocky lane up to Bodega Ruiz from the dual carriageway. We drove under a faded entrance sign of a wine bottle and a bunch of grapes into a car park. Lush dripping ferns and trees of prickly pears overflowed onto an assortment of rusting tractors and trailers. We sat in silence, our breath steaming the windows as the rain hollowed the roof of the car. I opened the car window to let in some fresh air and saw that Abba had dozed off, his eyes half open, a layer of crust on his lips.

A dog barked in the distance.

"Jesus" I cried, as a German Shepherd jumped up to the window of the car. A weathered elderly man followed, wearing a waterproof jacket that hung from his barrel like shoulders. A torn cowboy hat sat askew on his head, and his belly fell over the top of his jeans, tight against an España 82' World Cup t-shirt.

"Diego," the man shouted, holding the dog by the collar.

"Hi," I said, staying close to the car as I got out. "Is it possible to do a wine tour?"

"*Lo siento*, I'm sorry. Not today."

He lifted his head towards the sky and shrugged.

"Maybe we can look around the vineyards, try some cheese?" I pointed to a picture in the leaflet Richard had given me of a plate of cheese.

"It's not the right season."

I looked at him quizzically.

"Can you recommend anything else we can do around here?"

"I'm not a tourist guide. Ask at your hotel. Where are you staying?"

"Hotel Optimist," I said. "Are you Mr Ruiz?" I asked desperately.

He nodded slowly at me.

"Do you know Richard? From Sun-Seekers? It was his idea to come."

"Oh Richard! You know what happened last time Richard was here? *Hijo de puta.*"

"Look, we're not a hen party. It's just my father and me."

Ruiz looked into the car. "OK," he sighed, "I'll show you the wine cellar. But you can tell Richard that this is the last time I do him any favours, OK?"

Abba and I followed Ruiz into a barn filled with rows of stainless steel casks. I stopped at a cabinet to look at a few yellowing photographs of a younger Ruiz, wearing the same hat, one arm slung around an older man, holding trophies and magnums of wine.

Abba gripped the handrail on one side and wrapped his other arm around my shoulders as we descended one step at a time into a cellar.

"The cellar," Ruiz declared. He pulled on a cord that lit a corridor of shelves stacked with bottles of wine. As the lights came on, one at a time, I noticed that the cellar walls close to where we were standing were covered with graffiti; hearts with arrows through them, names, cities and countries, acid face smilies and anarchy symbols. I thought of adding 'holiday with Abba 2006'.

"My family has lived on this Bodega for three hundred years, and has been making wine all that time," Ruiz continued, a silver tooth twinkling in the light. "Now, there's too much rain. The wine isn't as good as it used to be." He took a bottle of red wine from a shelf and dusted it with the sleeve of his jacket. "You see this one?" he asked, showing Abba and I the bottle. "I won the 'Best Wine in Tenerife' prize for this in 1985. Now, no one wants to buy it. Tourists only want to drink these days."

"Any chance of a taste?" Abba asked.

"You can buy a bottle upstairs."

"But the leaflet says that you can try the wine on the tour."

"*Señor*, you buy the wine and then, you taste the wine."

Diego barked at my feet.

We sat at the end of an oak table while Ruiz shined a couple of wine glasses.

"*Listán Negro*, 2002, very young," he said, and poured two generous measures.

"*L'Chaim*," Abba said, his hand slowly lifting the glass to his mouth. He sank into his chair.

The wine was toasty, thick with sleep. Ruiz left us a basket of salty crackers and a plate with slices of *salchichón*. Abba drained his first glass, then started to help himself to another, the bottle shaking in his hand. I took it from him and finished pouring. "Go on, top it up," he said.

I looked at Abba as he almost inhaled the wine. To him, this wasn't what he called 'real drinking'. That was done in pubs, and pubs were full of yobbos who pissed on pavements. Pubs didn't sell decent wine, only pints and they were stuffed with smoke. Pub food was lathered in ketchup and mayonnaise and stank of vinegar, and the music was loud and pop-ey.

From an early age I'd seen him drink before dinner, with dinner, after dinner. Before the theatre. After the theatre. After work. Before bedtime. Sometimes with lunch. On holiday. At family gatherings. After a walk. When he felt like it. While listening to music. While watching the news. After a snooze. Before driving. "Come on, let's take a taxi home, we can get the car tomorrow," my mother would remonstrate with him after a meal out. "To hell with it, the police have better things to do than worry about me," he'd insist and take the wheel of the car.

And then there was the time Abba came home late after a meal with friends when I was six or seven. His weight sunk onto the mattress of my bed as he woke me to say good night. My eyes focused on his that rolled in his head. He smelt of cheese. His breath was win-ey. I curled under my duvet. "Come on... a cuddle for Abba," he said, forcing his arms under my body, lifting me towards him and kissing my head. "Leave him, he's sleeping," my mother called from downstairs. "I'm only saying goodnight..." Abba cried. "It's past midnight for God's sake, leave him alone," she shouted. I yawned. He gripped me tighter, rubbing his stubble against my face like an animal searching for affection, and dozed on me for a few minutes, his chest rising and falling onto mine, his mouth drooling. "*Laila tov*, good night my son," he said, eventually releasing me. "Can you leave the hall light on?" I asked, but everything was plunged into darkness as the floorboards outside my door creaked under his weight. I snuck out of my bedroom to turn the light back on, but as I did heard heated arguments from downstairs, so I sat down against the frame of my bedroom door. With the lights on it felt safer there. I always hoped that someone would find me

86

and carry me back to bed, but they never did, so eventually I'd crawl back into my room and fall asleep, the continuing shouts from downstairs ringing in my ears.

No, this wasn't real drinking.

Ruiz joined us at the table. "What do you think?" he asked.

"It's dry, isn't it?" I asked.

Abba smiled at Ruiz.

"Where you from?"

"Ireland. Well, I live in... it doesn't matter. Ireland," I said.

"I like Ireland. Nice people. Generous people."

"Not everyone's nice," Abba interrupted.

"Of course, *señor*, but the ones that come to my Bodega are nice, no?"

"If you say so."

"Apart from the hens?" I said.

Ruiz laughed as he tore a piece of *salchichón* with his stubby fingers. "It goes well with this wine. Don't you like it?"

"Thanks, but... ehhh... we're Jewish..."

"Oh, oh, *lo siento*. I'll bring you some cheese."

I put my feet on the chair left vacant by Ruiz and let the earthy tannins fill the pores of my mouth. A mosquito buzzed like a dive bomber next to my ear and flew in front of my eye-line. I swiped at it, clenching my fist, but it flew away and buzzed in the other ear. My chair rocked forward as I threw my hand in front of my head again, nearly knocking over the bottle of wine. The mosquito landed on my arm. I crushed it with my thumb, its blood bursting on my skin.

"Have you finished Roth?" I asked Abba.

"I'm onto Zweig, *The World of Yesterday*. Started it last night. It's marvellous." He paused. "You know they committed suicide?"

I shook my head.

"Zweig and his wife." Abba licked his lips and took another sip. "Couldn't take it anymore. Imagine. He'd survived the early part of the war, got all the way to Brazil with his wife and then…" Abba motioned to slice his neck.

"That's a bit of an extreme reaction, don't you think? I mean, didn't he want to just enjoy himself. I wouldn't mind being in Brazil."

"He'd had enough. He could do what the hell he wanted. He was a free man. He'd said what he had to say. No one listened to him anymore. No one paid him any attention. No one read his work. He was hounded like a criminal out of Europe. They destroyed his writings, his house, his life. The town he grew up in was bombed. There was nothing left. What was he expected to do? Lie on Copacabana beach for the rest of his life, get a tan and drink cocktails? Incredible when you think about it. A Jew. A Jew committing suicide, after surviving all that. Just incredible."

Abba snapped a cracker. "Maybe I should do that?"

"Don't be ridiculous."

"Why not? What's there to live for?"

"Oh, I don't know. Your wife, your family, your friends, your work, me."

"Yes, yes, I know that…" he said, waving his hand at me. "But what's there to *really* live for? Like *really*? There's no culture anymore. That's what Zweig says. We left it behind. Ruined it. Years ago. What's actually left?"

"What do you mean? Things are allowed to change you know."

"Yes, but it's not the same, nothing's the same."

"*Señores, queso de cabra*," Ruiz said, placing a wooden plate on the table with slices of goat's cheese dotted with tiny holes. He re-filled our glasses. Abba went off to pee.

"You know," Abba cleared his throat as he returned to the table. "I was once told by my boss at RTÉ that I couldn't be expected to know much about Irish affairs. You know why?"

I'd heard this story before.

"Because I was Jewish. Not Irish."

"That must have been hard to hear." I went with him.

"I was bloody furious." He drained his second glass. "Furious. After all that I'd done for that bloody television station. Antisemitism. Pure and simple."

"Surely just stupidity."

"No, no, she wasn't stupid," he said. "Just bloody ignorant."

"Do you think she thought that you can't be Irish and Jewish?"

"She had no idea what it meant for me, for me," he said, jabbing his chest with his finger, "to be Jewish. She didn't even ask."

"How could she have known if you didn't tell her?"

"At least be sensitive to it? No? She knew I was Jewish."

He bit into some cheese.

"So… there you have it," he said.

"There you have what?"

"That's it."

"But how did it make you feel?"

Come on, I thought, he brought it up.

"I just got on with it," Abba said. "I didn't have a choice. I wanted to get some programmes made, so I had to take it. But

89

this nonsense that all the Irish are friendly and generous and this and that…"

"Why didn't you say something?"

"What *could* I say?"

"That you thought it was offensive."

"Are you listening? It wasn't an option."

"Why not? Why didn't you ask her what she meant?"

"Look, can you stop asking me all these questions. I've told you what she said. I don't know the answers." He removed his glasses and rubbed his face.

"I suppose I don't understand. Why didn't you stick up for yourself? Who cares about the programmes? We would have still loved you, even if you hadn't made them."

"It was my work. My life."

"And what about the rest of us?"

"What about the rest of…" Abba made a halt sign with his hand. His bloodshot eyes were filled with tears. I'd taken it too far.

We moved to a metal table that Ruiz had wiped dry under a twisting wisteria in the garden. The rain had lifted and warm afternoon sunlight lit the gravelly terrace. Abba devoured the cheese as well as the rind and drank the rest of his wine in silence. I helped myself to another glass, closed my eyes and let the sun heat the back of my neck.

"*Otra botella*? Another bottle?" Ruiz asked. Diego sniffed my crotch.

"To hell with it. One more," Abba said.

Ruiz returned with another carafe. "*Malvasia*, a Bodega speciality. We only produce a few bottles a year. 2004 was a good year for the *Malvasia*, lots of sun, only a little rain. Now, it's the other way around, too much rain and not enough sun."

I pressed the car horn a bit too firmly as I drove off. Holding the steering wheel with one hand, I pulled the seat belt over my chest and plugged it in. Diego ran after the Cinquecento, barking and snapping at the wheels as we bumped down the rocky lane. Branches from overhanging trees skidded along the roof of the car. I was fizzy. With one eye on the road, I removed my sandals and curled the tips of my toes against the pedals, my heels resting on the gritty floor mat.

The single-lane tarmac road shimmered in the afternoon heat. It opened up like curvaceous liquorice, cutting through the volcanic landscape of red clay. Warm air rushed against my face as I changed gears effortlessly up and down, driving close to the cars in front as I nipped in and around slow drivers admiring the view.

There was a wildness in my veins. The car cut through a crosswind as I edged it onto the cracked sloped verge and treated the road like a racetrack. Shifting into the centre of the road, the powerful pull of the clutch on my leg, I sped round a bend, ignoring the speed limit, my lips crackly, my mouth dry, my eyes wide open. Entering a tunnel, I squinted behind my sunglasses, trying to make the road as dark as possible. The only lights visible were the cat's eyes, blinking at me, telling me to slow down. I closed my eyes momentarily. How far did I dare drive without looking? I was floating in the car, my limbs working independently, my head being pulled away from my skull. We emerged out of the tunnel as the road converged with nature, the sound of the tyres breaking the asphalt, the sun beating the windscreen.

Fiddling with the radio, I found some crackly classical music and looked over at Abba. His forearm rested on the open window, the passenger seat was pushed back. He had a still, content look on his face.

The streets of Dublin were Abba's open road. He'd accelerate quickly up to fourth or fifth gear, as if he needed to speed away from something. He'd dart in front of other cars and take corners at speed. His feet would caress the biting point on the clutch and accelerator at traffic lights before whizzing off, bossing the fast lane, flashing at "bloody women drivers." The swerves and screeches would scare yet exhilarate me when I was younger. They still did. He never crashed.

Diesel fumes filled the car as it struggled to climb a steep pass behind a slow-moving lorry, petrol dripping from its exhaust. I pulled over at a windy viewpoint to let Abba pee. At the top of the vista, with a view of Volcan Tiede, a tall white metal cross rose into the blue sky, glistening against the now blazing sun. Notes had been thumbtacked onto it, some covered in plastic, a few now blank where the writing had washed away. Others had fallen and were scattered on shingle, like the slips of paper that visitors leave at the Wailing Wall in Jerusalem; thousands are squeezed into the cracks of the smooth rectangular boulders every day, people hoping that their wishes, desires and questions are read by someone, somewhere and that everything will turn out OK.

Offerings of bottles of fizzy drinks, unopened packets of biscuits, pieces of costume jewellery and photographs of children littered the ground around the cross. A pair of crutches and a prosthetic leg were leaning against an abandoned wheelchair. Maybe I could leave a bottle of wine, or pin my questions wrapped in plastic film to the cross and let the ink weather away in the dry wind, that way I wouldn't have to bother.

"Shall we?" I asked, as we watched an aeroplane thunder overhead, make a sharp turn then straighten up before lining up to land.

"I need a snooze," Abba said.

The road widened as I joined a rush of traffic entering Playa de las Américas. We drove along the coast road as long afternoon shadows flickered in and out of the car, like a Super 8 film. Parking in the hotel car park I stirred Abba awake, realising he'd left his seat belt undone.

"How's my man Ruiz?" Richard asked from behind his desk. "Did you get a discount?"

I'd forgotten about the discount.

"Do you think he's forgiven me?"

"We were the only ones there." I needed coffee.

Abba had walked off to the bar.

"Are you alright?" Richard asked.

"Just hot." I needed paracetamol.

"How's your dad?"

"He's having a drink." I needed a cigarette.

Richard's basketball trainers squeaked as he stood up and looked down at me.

"If you want to get away from him, just let me know. There's plenty you can do without him. I can arrange things…" he said, nodding, as if agreeing with himself.

"Arrange things?"

"Yeh, you know," he said, "like para gliding or surfing, or something like that."

"Oh," I said, almost disappointed.

"I know, why don't you join me on my favourite event of the week. Richie's Famous Mid-Week Pub Crawl. Seven pubs in seventy minutes, leaving at seven o'clock. Do you see what I did there?" he laughed. "It's deadly. Pint and shot in every pub. If you make it to the end, and not many do, you get a free t-shirt, designed by yours truly! Most of the lads don't make it to the end, but the girls, they're brilliant at it. And wait till you see them the next morning! It's only thirty euros and that covers everything, including free entry into Ver-o-ni-ca's," he sang as he swayed his hips.

"I'll eh, think about it."

"Well, you know where I am if you need me."

Richard sat down at his desk, opened a laptop and started to type. I stared down at him and craned my head to see what he was doing. He looked up briefly, catching me unawares, and returned to his work. I turned my head and peered through the open doors to the bar and saw Abba sitting unsteadily on a stool nursing a whiskey. I motioned to go and join him, afraid that he'd fall over, but my legs wouldn't move. I stared intensely at Richard, willing him to say something, but all I could hear was his finger turning the roller ball of his mouse. I wanted him to say something, to ask me about me, to distract me. What was he doing that was so important? He didn't have much to do. Why didn't he want to talk to me?

…I'm off to London tomorrow for meetings. I can't say that I'm looking forward to it. It's extremely hot there and the idea of London in the heat is not appealing. Glad to see you're reading Nietzsche. I did have a book of his essays, but I lent it to someone and that was the end of it… how's that for negative philosophy?

DAY FIVE

Homesick

I woke from a nightmare in agony, my right arm bloodless and limp, as if I'd slept on it. Disorientated, clammy and short of breath, I thought I heard faint knocking on the door of the apartment. I ignored it. Everything in my room seemed unfamiliar; the single bed, lumpy pillows, wicker lampshade, blackout curtains. Disconnected images came back to me. A creaking aeroplane crashing into the north Atlantic. Trays of airplane food, life jackets and sachets of Bullseye whiskey floating in the flooded cabin. Shards of sunlight piercing the dark water. Abba and I the only passengers left on board, sitting patiently in our seats waiting to be rescued, our seat belts fastened, holding hands and singing *Kaddish*, the mourner's prayer. My questions drifting past me in the water, desperately swiping at them, trying to catch them, but missing every time, the words on the page fading in the light, the folded piece of paper disappearing among the debris. Another knock. This time louder. I sat up. Blood eased back into my arm, warming my tingling flesh. Turning on the light on my bedside table I saw *Herzog* and my wallet. I remembered. Tenerife, with Abba.

I opened the door. A youthful looking woman dressed in tracksuit bottoms and trainers appeared from behind a trolley stacked with towels, mops, cloths, bottles of shampoo, dusters and sheets. A necklace hung from her neck with the name Ines carved on a gold pendant, and her hair was tied in a bun that was tightly wrapped in a hair net.

"Good morning. Cleaning service," she said, showing off a brace on her lower set of teeth.

"OK… wait a sec, I'll be back in a minute."

"Abba," I whispered, kneeling on the floor, next to his bed. I smelt his sleepy breath.

He woke sluggishly, licked his lips, and hoisted himself up to a seated position.

"The cleaning lady's here, and it's breakfast time," I said.

"Now? The place doesn't need a clean," he said yawning.

"She says she has to do it today."

"Give me five minutes."

Ines pushed her trolley into the apartment, trying to avoid bumping it against the edges of the walls.

"Your father?" she asked as she unloaded fresh towels and sheets.

"Yes," I said, sitting on the arm of the sofa.

"Holiday?"

I nodded.

"He's old, no?"

Richard must have briefed her.

"I don't think he'd like it if I called him old."

"My father's also old. He never wants to go on holiday. He's so difficult. Always this or that. My parents argue all the time, so they stay at home. It's nice of you to go away with your father."

I didn't respond.

"Do you have children?" she asked.

"No, you?"

"A boy. Rafael," she said, and held up a cracked mobile phone with a picture of a chubby toddler with curly hair.

I leant forward to get a closer look. "Sweet. You from Tenerife?" I asked.

"Playa, all my life."

"Do you like it?"

"It's OK, but one day I'd like to go on holiday."

"How long have you worked at the hotel?"

"Three years. Since I finished school. My mother also works here, in the kitchen."

"What's it like, working here?" I wasn't sure what I meant. Was I trying to get into a discussion about how the hotel treats its staff? Or maybe, I was just keen to prolong the feeling of having a normal everyday conversation with someone new and unfamiliar.

"You ask a lot of questions, huh?" Ines asked with her back to me.

"Sometimes..."

"What do you do?"

My breath tightened. I didn't know how to explain what I did. Afterall I wasn't sure anymore. I was between jobs, and still debating what to do next. Trying to explain public relations to someone just seemed too hard. It wasn't interesting. I wasn't interested in it. I wasn't even sure why I'd spent so many years writing about and promoting companies that I couldn't care less about and that did little for the world apart from exploit it. I had questioned for a while what I was doing and what I was doing it for, but was stuck, in some kind of limbo where I felt I needed to work and earn money but found it hard to be truthful about what I really wanted to do, whatever that was. So I told her I worked in advertising. At least that way she'd know what I meant, and I wouldn't have to explain myself.

"And your father?" she asked.

"He doesn't work anymore, but he used to make television programmes and plays. Once, I don't remember when, he directed a Samuel Beckett play in front of the great man. He claims he was too shy to introduce himself after the show," I laughed, "and he made this documentary about child abuse in Ireland that was talked about in the Irish parliament, and the first ever programme on Israeli television…"

Ines turned from the mantelpiece and raised her chin. I paused, realising that somehow, I always ended up talking about Abba's life and work rather than mine in conversation, often without hesitation. He stood behind me in his dressing gown. Barefoot, unshaven, his eyes squinting, he looked like he'd crumpled in on himself in the night.

"Well at least someone remembers what I did," Abba said. "Can you get me a bottle of cold water from downstairs?" he asked. "There's a good man."

"You OK?" I asked.

"I'm fine," he sighed. "I just feel a bit, sticky."

A coachload of newly arrived tourists milled around the hotel lobby with suitcases and holdalls, busily checking in. Richard was directing a group of women wearing cowboy hats with tassels and pink t-shirts to the bar and a family of four towards our part of the hotel. I had a sudden urge to be swept away with the crowd so I stood for a few minutes in the middle of the throng, and let people knock past me, slapping my back and legs with their bulging bags.

Heat warmed my bare feet on the pavement. I took two bottles of cold water from the fridge of the kiosk outside the hotel and paid. A stray black mastiff with matted hair slept on the edge of the pavement. I crouched next to her; the thick fur of her body warm in my hand. As I stroked the dog she snored quietly, her belly gently rising and falling, her tongue thick with bubbles of saliva hanging from her open mouth. I watched a file of ants trail around the dog's body along the edge of the pavement into a drain. A taxi approached the hotel and stopped abruptly by the pavement. Car doors slammed, waking the dog. She vigorously scratched her head and body, disturbing the ants there, and then limped away into the sun, off to find another spot to be left alone.

"Ah, good man, what took you?" Abba asked as I returned to the apartment.

"Why haven't you got dressed yet?"

"I was about to, but thought Ines here could do with the company."

Abba drank from a bottle of water, some spilling onto his chest. He then shuffled towards the bedroom cradling his hernia, grabbed onto the back of a chair and aimlessly clawed the wall every few steps for support.

"We were just talking about Israel," Abba said, as he returned to the lounge, and sat next to me.

"Come on, let's go to breakfast," I said.

"I dreamt I was back there and asked Ines if she'd been, and told her how marvellous it is."

"She doesn't need to hear that. Thanks Ines, see you around," I said.

"Why not?"

"You *know* why not," I said despondently.

"She can answer for herself you know."

"It sounds so beautiful," Ines said, looking up from scrubbing the kitchen sink. "I've not been. Maybe one day I'll go with my son. But his father never wants to go anywhere. How do you say? He gets, homesick?"

"Yeh, homesick," I said. I felt I was correcting her.

"He gets homesick," Ines said slowly, "so we don't go anywhere. We stay here, with the hotel, and his mother, and his friends… It's OK." She stared straight through me, a lonely look in her eyes, then pulled the cord out of the Henry Hoover, plugged it into the wall and stamped on the power, drowning us out of the room.

Abba and I sat in a quiet corner of the hotel breakfast hall. He tried to open a portion of butter. I took it from him and unwrapped the greasy foil using the tip of my knife.

"Why don't you ever want to talk about Israel?" he asked, spreading the fingers of his hands.

"Because I might have other things I want to talk about," I muttered.

"Bloody things, what's wrong with good old-fashioned blocks of butter," Abba grunted as he spread his toast. "I woke up feeling that we should have gone there instead of here. There's nothing to do here, and there's not enough heat."

"It's pretty hot today," I said, hoping that would please him.

"Answer the question," Abba insisted.

"Because."

"Is that all you have to say?"

"Don't you think we've talked about it enough?" I asked. This was not the conversation I wanted to have.

"Not recently."

"I meant in the past. And anyway, I don't think the cleaning lady was interested."

"I was only trying to be friendly."

"It was your idea to come here. I'd have gone anywhere."

"Your mother wouldn't have gone to Israel."

"Possibly. But she's not here."

"She refuses to talk about it anymore. Says I pick fights with her, when in fact she's the one that picks the fight. I just want to have a discussion," he said, placing his knife firmly down on the table. "Now you, you also want to censor me. Everyone censors me. I'm never allowed to say what I want."

"No one is denying you your rights, we just don't need to hear it every, single, day."

"But it's important. To me!"

"Well, I'm sure you can find some kind of Zionist self-help group to go to if you feel that strongly about it," I said, and went to refill our coffee cups, never understanding why hotel cups are always so shallow and the coffee luke-warm.

"What could be more important than the future of our homeland, *der heym*?" Abba asked, as I returned to the table.

"It's not my homeland and I don't think it's yours."

"*Be-emet*... really?"

"Why would I call it my homeland?"

"Why wouldn't you? You spent enough time there as a child. I thought you liked it."

"I don't know where my home is anymore. It doesn't matter."

"But you're Jewish."

"So?"

"What do you mean 'so'? Isn't Israel important to you?"

"If it's so important to you, why didn't you stay there when you had the chance?"

"You know it was impossible. We've been over this. I would have loved to, but, I suppose I was…"

"What?"

"I found it hard, OK? And anyway, your mother didn't want to stay. It's too late now. She'd never go back, bloody hates the place." He paused. "I just thought you'd… ahhh, it doesn't matter."

"What doesn't matter?"

"Nothing. I just thought we could talk about it," he said, scrunching up his face. "I thought that you, of *all* people, were on my side?"

"Does it really still matter whose side I'm on?"

Half an hour later, I pushed two chairs together along the paving stones by the pool and placed our coffee cups on a table.

Abba asked if I could help him with some eye drops, so like a parent with a newborn, I held his head in one hand and lightly squeezed the bottle of solution, letting two drops fall onto each eye. They glistened under the saline.

"What would you like to do today?" I asked.

"Ahhh, the sun, it's marvellous. My legs are killing me."

I hung my feet in the cool water of the pool noticing how pale they looked in contrast to my now tanned legs. Despite the heat, goosebumps covered the tops of my thighs and arms. My breath was shallow. I raised my head to Richard as he walked towards the Mexican-themed pool bar. He ignored me, and high-fived the bar man, who was busily arranging his station, waiting for the day's first order of Piña Coladas.

Every summer until my late teens, my mother took my sister and I to Israel to visit family, usually without Abba. My grandmother's first floor apartment in Haifa was my favourite place in the world, my hideaway, my retreat from the draughty house in Dublin I was brought up in. Because she never fully opened the plastic shutters, the floor tiles were always cold, the corridors dark. For some reason she liked it that way. Maybe she didn't want anyone to see in, or for her to see out. Most evenings she'd sit at the dining table and talk to her friends on the telephone in a mixture of German and Hebrew, pausing every few moments to cough violently from the Time cigarettes she smoked. I loved the thick smell of tobacco that lifted from her red lipstick- stained cigarette butts and schnitzel sizzling in a greasy frying pan in her sparse kitchen, the tar that stuck to my sandals on the pavement, the grumbling buses, the pine needles that caught between my toes, and the sticky fruit on sale in the grocery store across the road.

I'd spend endless days on the beach with my cousins getting tanned with no sunscreen, eating bubble gum flavoured ice-cream, often returning to my grandmother's apartment on the last bus. As the youngest, I was dared to slot pornographic playing cards under my grandmother's elderly neighbour's door, hide, and run as Mrs Fishbein unlocked her door and stumbled after me waving her broom. Late into the night, my cousins and I would pretend to get drunk on non-alcoholic beer and tiptoe into my grandmother's bedroom, and giggle uncontrollably while listening to her epic snores. In the evenings I'd stretch out on the scratchy sofa and watch a Western with her on her knackered black and white television, the sound turned up high, eating falafel and cold chips, and drinking chocolate milk.

I never knew why Abba didn't come on these trips, apart from one summer when he just showed up. After a month of not seeing him, there he was, no warning, no announcement. Who was this pale stranger in khaki shorts and canvas boots? Would I have to revert to speaking English rather than Hebrew, and do as I was told? Would we still be allowed to go to the beach, eat bubblegum ice-cream, watch Westerns? My mother, sister and I danced around him for a few days. I hid the playing cards.

He didn't stay for long, but long enough for him to take me on a day trip to Akko in the north of the country. We walked around the Arab town without saying much, nibbling on freshly baked bageles covered in sesame seeds and za-atar. "You can't come to Akko and not have fish", he told me, so we ate grilled trout with pickled peppers and tahini at a busy seafood restaurant by the harbour. The evening journey back to Haifa was dusty, the two of us the only passengers in a bus that trumped along the coast road. Abba put his hand over my shoulders and held on to me as we sat on metal seats, the windows open, the sultry evening air rushing onto our faces and peeling shoulders, the warmth of his body against mine. It was the happiest I ever was with him. I was asleep when he left the next morning. I didn't see him for another month.

During those years Abba would sometimes gather us in my bedroom in our house in Dublin for one of his many slide shows. He'd hang a sheet on the wardrobe door and point the projector at it, a growl howling from the motor. One of the many trays of black and white or colour slides he'd shot during his time in Israel would then click into place. We'd sit on the floor, and I'd make shapes with my hand onto the screen, as motes of dust twinkled in the bright light.

It was my job to press the control that moved the slides around the carousel with a firm click. I always tried to skip the endless shots of the archaeological sites of Masada or Caesarea and find the embarrassing photographs of Abba with an ex-girlfriend. But he liked to pause on grainy images of him next to his Fiat Spitfire that he drove around Israel, drinking coffee in cafes on pedestrianised streets and sunning himself by the beach. Cold, wet Ireland was replaced by the joys of the sea breeze, fresh food, and the freedom to do what he wanted, when he wanted.

Abba would tell the same story on those nights. How he left Ireland in 1967 to fight in the Six-Day War in Israel. How he took the slow route and drove his Spitfire across Europe to the Middle-East, by which time he'd seen the sights of Rome, Athens, Istanbul, Crete and Cyprus. How he arrived too late to be useful to the war effort, which had finished weeks before. How he loved watching films at the Cinémathèque in Jerusalem, eating *me'orav Yerushalmi*, mixed Jerusalem grill, and walking on the walls of the Old City. How he could drive to Hebron, visit the Temple

Mount; there was none of the security restrictions there are now.
How he wrote to his mother and told them he was working and
that he was well. How his mother would respond with news of
his sisters and brother, always signing-off, 'Affectionately yours,
your mother.' How he always said, 'Affectionately yours, your
mother,' with a sadness in his eyes.

I'd watch slack-jawed for a couple of hours as I clicked
through endless slides and film clips of Abba giving directions
to cameramen on Israeli television productions, such as the first
Israeli Independence Day Parade to be televised in 1968. He
struggled to learn Hebrew, so often confused words, making his
workmates laugh with strange pronunciations that he'd learnt
bent over a prayerbook at Hebrew classes as a child every Sunday
morning. Even though his Hebrew was limited, he knew enough
to understand what was going on, what was being said about
this Irishman behind his back, what they really thought of him.
Thinking they knew better, they stopped listening to him, didn't
follow his instructions, avoided his scripts and ignored him.

"Come on, one more ream," he said one evening. The label
read 'Kineret-67'; a trip to Lake Kineret, with Abba's parents-
in-law and my mother. His running commentary. "Oh, there I
am again by the car. Glorious sunset. Yes, the food wasn't great
was it? There's your grandmother. What's she reading? Oh, the
Joyce I gave her. Oh, yes, the log cabin we all shared. There's me,
trying to cool down. Bloody hell it was hot. I stayed in the water
for three days, ha, ha. And your grandfather painting, he was
bloody good you know. Ah, yes, me again, with a glass of wine.
Ha! Christ it was hard to sleep. I had to change in the toilets,
do you remember?" he asked my mother. She nodded. "There's

the rest of you going off for a walk. I don't think I went. There's me again. Group shot. I couldn't cool down. Didn't you find it embarrassing that I had to change in front of your parents? Gosh, I was breathless. Even the wine tasted off to me. Yep, I saw your father's doc about my ticker after that weekend. He gave me some pills and told me to slow down." My mother nodded. Then a blank slide. Another. A slide of my mother with her parents. Another blank. One of Abba reading. Another blank. Another blank. "Enough," he said. I turned off the projector, the whirring of the motor growing more intense as the bulb faded, all of us left in darkness staring at the blank sheet in front of us.

Abba struggled on working in Israel for a few months after that, and eventually decided that he couldn't make it work. In 1972 he returned to the comfort of Ireland with his new Israeli wife, my mother.

The skin on my feet had turned wrinkly in the pool. I couldn't settle my mind on one thing. The big questions, little questions, seemingly inconsequential questions on the piece of paper I'd brought with me. The endless fraught family arguments, usually about Israel, who was right and who was wrong, and which side you were on gripped our family like a vice. So much so that I wasn't quite sure myself.

I hated family arguments, and always wanted to find the peace. I was nicknamed 'the diplomat' by my family when I was young. I'd sit on the side lines, always feeling a bit part in a bigger performance that was being played out in front of me, night after night, week after week. My minor role left me feeling indecisive, tentative, unable to express what I really felt. I always seemed to only have a few, insignificant lines.

The pressure of living with a cultured, creative, yet complicated man intensified the older I got. As Abba lurched from one television production to another, and one health scare to another, I'd often hold my breath in his presence, not knowing what to do around him.

"Will you stop following me," he'd say, and turn and glare at me standing on the stairs of our house, as I trailed him like a dog looking for attention.

Yet I loved him, constantly yearning for his affection as I grew up. I needed to impress him whichever way I could. Sometimes, I'd cautiously ask him for help with my homework. Surely he'd want to help me with *Macbeth*, his favourite Shakespeare. "I can't understand a word of this," he'd say, "and why are you using blue and green ink? You can't do that in an exam, and get some bloody handwriting lessons while you're at it."

The need to know some answers crept up in me as I grew older. Abba seemed so distant to me in so many ways. There was too much left unanswered, unsaid. Why did he just turn up in Haifa that summer? Why was he so angry so often? Why did he constantly blame my mother? He called her co-counselling group the 'cows of feminism', and when she went on a weekend away with them sometime in the 1980s, he shouted and scrunched up his face and eyes as he cried on my shoulder, begging for my mother's return, blaming the other women for wrenching her from his grasp. He called me his 'only friend', his 'best friend'. He wanted to be my friend 'for life'. I had no idea what he was saying. He seemed so alone, so vacant. I was voiceless against his lament.

…As if last week wasn't bad enough, some bloody Trinity students, and you know what Joyce said about Trinity students… well never mind… pas devants les enfants, pocketed the keys to the pottery studio and walked away with them, so I couldn't pot on Saturday. Some of that lot make my clay curdle…

Veronica's

"I'm going out tonight," I said, while eating lunch on a stool at the pool bar.

"You're abandoning me?" Abba asked, biting into a cheese toastie.

"That's right."

"Who with?"

"Richard."

"You think he'll make better conversation than me?"

"I won't be back late."

"Well make sure you don't get into any trouble. You should hear the shouting and the screaming that goes on every night outside my room."

"You coming later?" Richard asked after walking across the sun drenched paving stones from the main pool and popping under the shade of the pool bar.

"Just for a few," I said.

"Deadly. We'll be in Hoorahans down on the beach from seven, but if we're not there, try La Fiesta, which is just down the road. We'll look after him don't worry now, Mr eh, Lentin, isn't it? How are you doing by the way?"

"Please, you're blocking the sun," Abba said, gesticulating at him to move.

"Alright, alright. I'll see you later." Richard pointed at me and marched off, rubbing his hands gleefully together.

"I can't believe you're leaving me, for him," Abba said.

"I'm not leaving you."

"How's *Herzog*?"

"I might give up," I said, knowing he'd be disappointed.

"What? You can't give up on Bellow. Stick with it, you might learn something."

"Yeh, how to be depressed..."

We finished munching on our toasties and a stingy bowl of fries and drank a couple of glasses of chilled Listán Blanco. A couple of lads ordered Mojitos from the barman and plugged a MiniDisc into the sound system that was at one end of the bar. Techno beats now filled the space that was occupied by Abba, me, and two lads in skimpy shorts dancing in the early afternoon sun.

'Richie's Famous Mid-Week Pub Crawl' was on its last legs. He'd taken a motley crew of a few couples, guys and girls in their late teens desperate to get away from their parents, two pensioners who liked to dance, the man I'd met under the table in the breakfast room while retrieving Abba's pills, and his girlfriend who I tried to avoid, and me. First stop, La Fiesta on the beach for pints, then Hoorahans' for shots, Frankie's Bar for more pints, Pooles for a cheeseburger and chips, Sound of Cream for a vodka luge, Tramps for cocktails and then onto Veronica's for 'La Finale', as Richard called it.

"You can't have wine on a pub crawl," Richard said, as I ordered at La Fiesta. "This isn't tea with your dad. Come on, you're getting a pint and a chaser," he insisted.

The rest of the group looked me up and down, in my polo t-shirt, chinos and sandals. I blew my nose into a handkerchief as I tried to engage in conversation with some of the lads about football but spent most of the evening hovering on the side lines, smirking about things I knew little about.

At first I didn't know why I'd gone, apart from the appeal of not spending another evening sitting across a dining table from Abba arguing about this or that. He told me that he'd be quite happy to go out alone, even fancied an early night, though I did fleetingly wonder if he'd found a decent restaurant and his way back to the hotel. But as the evening wore on, I enjoyed the feeling that he seemed further and further away from me, as if I was on holiday by myself, free for a short while.

"You Irish?" one of the lads, Joe, asked as we downed tequila shots in Tramps.

"Yeh," I responded suspiciously.

"You don't sound very Irish," he said. A few other lads he was with nodded.

"My father's Irish and my mother's Israeli. I live in London, so my accent's nearly gone." A mist of sweat edged through the pores of my forehead. I cracked the knuckles on my fingers.

"Are you sure?" Joe continued. "Where did you go to school?"

"Stratford College, Rathgar," I said.

"Ohhh, Rath-gar," Joe quipped, accentuating the 'g', laughing to the others, "South-sider! Posh part of town."

"My parents still live in Dublin… my accent comes out after I've had a few drinks." I let out a strained laugh.

"Really?" Joe asked. "You sound like, I don't know, where do you think he sounds like he's from?" he asked the group.

They paused.

"Nowhere," one of them said eventually, laughing and spitting out some of his drink. They all cracked up. I smiled.

"Will you leave him alone," Richard said, coming to my rescue.

"We're only pulling your leg," Joe said. He slapped me on the back and held his eye on me for a second. "Fancy another?" he asked.

Veronica's club was fleshy. Bare-chested men and women wearing bikini tops were sardined next to each other, flowing in unison in a wave around the DJ. The bar was five people deep with arms reaching out, notes at the ready, ordering pints, shots and cocktails from barmen spinning and catching bottles. I'd found the two pills I'd kept from Abba's pill pot in the pocket of my trousers. Without thinking I'd downed them with a mouthful of beer. Everything seemed heightened and vivid. Drenched in sweat, I was anxious. My heart pulsed in my temple. Thick walls of bass bounced around the cavern space, pulsating the low ceilings and sweat covered walls, sending deep reverberations around my ribs. Every few minutes, the music would pause, relaxing the crowd, before crashing through the mammoth speakers again, the dance floor exploding en-masse to the beat.

I stood alone in a corner of Veronica's, my t-shirt stuck against the wall. Moisture ran down my pint glass which I held against my forehead, the feeling cool on my clammy skin. *Easy*, I thought, as I pushed open the toilet door a bit too aggressively. It rebounded against a condom machine on the wall. I left my pint on the edge of the sink alongside other half empty glasses, sodden tissue and pink soap residue. I looked at myself in the dark mirror and stretched my mouth wide. My beard had grown, my face was tanned, my body tense from the alcohol. I held my phone in one hand and checked to see if Abba had texted, then balanced it on the wall of the urinal, always a dangerous occupation, but satisfying when I got it right. There was nothing. The hotel had my number in case there was an emergency, so I presumed everything was ok. As I peed, I leant my head against the greasy tiles in front of me and felt my body drain. A momentary urge to wipe away the congealed slime in the sink came over me, but I walked away. It was too disgusting.

"Fucking hell, there you are," a bare-chested Richard shouted in my ear as I returned to the bar. "I've been looking everywhere for you. I have a duty of care and all that, for my customers you know."

He smelled of coconut oil.

"Havin' fun?" he asked.

"Yeh, it's great," I said half-heartedly.

"Come on, dance with us." Richard grabbed my arm.

"I'm not much of a dancer."

"You don't have to be, it's just a good laugh."

"I'm fine," I said, wanting the conversation to end, my head cloudy.

"Well if you're not going to dance, you and me are having a shot."

Richard pushed his way to the front of the bar. Two shot glasses arrived on a silver tray. A blue flame circled the rim of the glass as it was lit by the barman who motioned to me to drink. Following Richard, I covered the glass with my hand to extinguish the flame and knocked it back. A burnt sweet alcoholic taste of caramel filled my throat like an oaky syrup.

"Woohoooo!" Richard cried and slapped me on the back as I coughed.

"Are you trying to kill me?"

"Jäger-bomb… Tenerife style, ha, ha."

I rested my elbows on the bar.

"You're very serious," Richard said, edging closer.

I pretended not to hear him.

"Something's going on between you and your dad, isn't it?"

I shook my head.

"Come on, you can talk to Uncle Richie. Your secret's safe with me."

"There's nothing to tell. We're on holiday, he's old, what more do you want me to say?"

"Suit yourself. Usually when people come on their holidays, they arrive all wound up. I see it all the time. But after a few days in the sun, I'm telling you, they're much more relaxed. You two though. You two are different. You seem to be getting more miserable."

"You try and talk to him then," I said, but as I spoke he turned to speak to a girl who had whipped his baseball cap off his head. I recognised her from the hotel. Ines, the cleaning lady, still wearing her pristine white trainers and holding her cracked mobile phone. They raised their eyes to me briefly as they talked, laughing with each other as they flicked through photos on their phones, an air of familiarity between them.

I left them. As I walked through a sea of bodies, my sandals crunched on broken glass and plastic cups. Kicking a few empty bottles of Smirnoff Ice that spun across the dance floor, I stood in the centre of the club and stopped. I closed my eyes. Joe was dancing in a circle with a few of the other lads, lightly bumping into me. The crowd edged aside as they danced in taunting circles. As the music intensified, I separated Joe's arm from the group and joined them. Gripping onto his shoulders we careered and jumped in unison. Lifting my knees up to my chest, I used Joe and the lad on my other side to hoist me higher and higher so I was now hovering over the ground, as if the music was sweeping me away. Some of the lads separated and started dancing alone or with some girls, but Joe and I continued. Arm in arm, we swung and twisted each other, spinning furiously, the strobe lights blending and blurring into one laser-like spotlight on us. Eventually I stopped, breathless, unable to focus, sweat dripping into my eyes and mouth, my head spinning as if it might come away from the rest of my body. I approached Joe and stood facing him closely for a few moments, my ears pounding, my eyes wide, his stubbly face in my line of sight.

"I am fucking Irish," I said aggressively, before turning and walking away.

The night air had cooled by the time I left Veronica's. The waves were breaking close to the shore. Pockets of revellers were milling outside the clubs, some shouting and screaming, others fiddling with cards in cashpoints, and a few sitting on the edge of pavements, heads between their legs. It was a short walk back to the Optimist, the salty sea air filling my lungs, the sounds of croaky karaoke drifting in the wind.

I slid across the marble floor of the bright hotel reception and noticed Abba sitting by the entrance to the bar, reading *The World of Yesterday*.

"Ah, you're back," he said.

"Why are you still up," I asked, surprised to see him. "It's nearly three A.M."

"I thought I'd wait up for you. I was just about to go to bed," he said, putting down his book. "I met a marvellous couple. O'Dwyers, I think they were called. Not sure. They invited me to dinner in the hotel."

"That's nice of them."

"I had paella."

"I thought we were going to have that on our last night?"

"Ah, to hell with it! I didn't fancy anything else."

"Any good?"

"A bit dry."

"I'm going to bed." I yawned, my head was pounding.

"We had a great conversation," Abba said as he picked up a brandy from the coffee table in front of him. I wondered how much he'd had to drink. "They agree with me."

"About what?"

"Israel."

"Great..." I mumbled and ran my hand over my head, pitying the O'Dwyers who probably thought they were doing a nice thing by inviting an old man alone to have dinner with them.

Abba finished his drink. "Right, I'm off to bed."

I watched him waddle to the lift, his flip flops flapping on the shiny floor, waving at the receptionists as he went. I followed him in the next lift, not wanting to be in his presence for a few moments. On floor three I found him wandering like a lost soul, flailing the walls for support as he walked down the wrong corridor, fumbling in his back pocket for the key-card to the apartment, his chinos flapping against his legs. Not wanting to surprise him, I walked up quietly behind him, held onto his arm and turned his body around, while holding onto his bloated waist. He moved with me as if he knew that I'd find and help him. His cheeks were flushed, his lips stained red, his breath garlicky. We walked arm-in-arm along the low-ceilinged corridor back to our room, safely enclosed by the walls, doors and flickering strip lights.

I helped Abba remove his stained blue sweatshirt and trousers, from which I picked off a few grains of dried rice. Lifting his legs one by one, I lay him onto his bed and covered him in a freshly starched white sheet. He fell asleep immediately.

I downed a couple of paracetamol and lit a cigarette. The smoke lifted me as I inhaled. My eyes danced over the pages of *Herzog* as I tried to read, turning the pages quickly, trying to sober up by focusing on a few words here and there. After a few pages, my mind slowed and I began to concentrate on the print, really concentrate as if I wanted to devour what he was saying so that I could remember it in the morning, even though I knew that I was drunk and that anything I read or thought of now would be gone, well gone by the time I woke up. Part of me wanted to drop the book and go back to the club, to Richard, to Ines, to the bar and just forget about it all, but I had to keep on going. I had an urge to lick the print so I could eat it up, take in all the pain and suffering Herzog was feeling and let it surge into me so I could understand what he was going through. If I did that maybe I'd understand Abba and maybe I'd understand myself.

...Actually you can count yourself lucky that I can write to you this evening, which I had reserved for this very purpose. Standing as I was in the kitchen, alone, the bloody carving knife, which I was using to cut through some meat from yesterday's roast, cut a large notch out of my index finger, the first one on the left hand. I never saw such blood since the bypass, actually I didn't see it then, which was just as well. Amazing the important events in life one misses! But the important thing is to be around to miss them!

DAY SEVEN

Bypass

I woke to a ringing in my ears. My head pounded. I was parched. I stepped into the shower, drew the plastic curtain that was dotted with spores of mould, and let hot water fall onto my head. The steam opened my pores and using a nail brush, I pummelled the soles of my feet and palms of my hands until they were bright red. I dug my nails into my scalp, wanting to remove a layer of my skin. It felt good to be alone, enveloped in a mass of mist. Standing in the shower I hugged my body, letting the water collect in my crossed arms, and watched it cascade onto my feet.

Feeling cleansed, I waited with Abba in the lobby of our floor for the lift to arrive, my stomach rumbling. "Doors opening," announced an electronic female voice. Abba rushed in, almost blocking the entrance, eager to get to breakfast. I followed, and stood against one side, gripping the wooden handrail. As the doors were about to kiss shut, they shuddered open again. A teenage girl with a perfectly cut fringe pushed past Abba, followed by Joe.

At first, we tried not to catch each other's eye, but despite our best efforts, every time we looked up, our faces reflected infinitely off the surrounding lift mirrors, as if we were still spinning in Veronica's. His stubble had thickened overnight, and he was wearing loose grey tracksuit bottoms, sliders and a Celtic football jersey. Abba refused to move as more people entered the lift that stopped at every floor. I shuffled towards the back and was now crammed in the corner alongside Joe. We turned our heads away from each other, and I detected a whiff of deodorant from him that he'd obviously sprayed over his clothes. Should I ask him how his head was, or apologise for my outburst the night before? But as I was about to speak, the lift doors opened and Joe and the girl squeezed their way out.

A cacophony of crockery, cutlery and chatter greeted us in the breakfast hall. The crowd moved rapidly between stainless steel servers, greedily piling their plates with fried breakfasts, as if they were all nursing hangovers. Joining the melee, I jostled for space, my arms rubbing against the skin of other guests. I felt a tap on my shoulder.

"Excuse me," an elderly woman with wispy red hair said. "Are you Lewis's son?" she asked.

"Lewis?" I turned to her, realising that she was the same woman I'd seen reading the bible by the pool.

"Yes, Lewis." It sounded like Lew-wis. "I'm sure that was his name. Are you his son?" She peered towards Abba, who was sitting at a table by the window.

"Yeh, that's me. It's Louis by the way." I needed coffee and didn't feel like making polite conversation.

"How is Lewis this morning?"

"Fine, I think, apart from the usual. Why?"

"I'm Mrs O'Dwyer."

She held out her hand to me. I gently squeezed it, trying not to crumple her bird-like fingers. "Lewis had dinner with us last night."

"Thanks for asking him. I was out, so…" My stomach groaned.

"Oh, it's no bother," she interrupted. "My husband, Tom, and I that is, enjoyed his company immensely. Such an interesting man. We were up for hours listening to him telling us stories about his work and his time abroad. All the things he's done. You're a lucky lad to have such a fascinating father." She coughed aggressively as if she was trying to release some phlegm at the back of her throat.

"Mind you, he doesn't mind a bit of drink now, wouldn't you say? And he got a bit upset you know, when talking…" She paused, reached up to my ear and whispered, "about the Holy Land."

"Really? That's very unlike him."

"He just started to cry. Not very much, but there were tears alright. I had to give him one of my tissues."

"Oh," I said, "it must have been his pills. They make him a bit weepy. I wouldn't worry. I've told him not to drink too much, but you know what a cocktail of pills and alcohol can do to you."

"But talking to your father brought back so many wonderful memories of the last time Tom and I went on pilgrimage, you know to Jerusalem, and Nazareth, and Hebron—"

"It was nice to…" I interrupted, and just as I started to walk away with a tray of food she dug her nails into my arm like claws and looked at me sternly with her piercing blue eyes.

"If he needs help, if he needs us, just give us the wink."

"I'll let him know."

I pushed my way to our table, sat down next to Abba and passed him half a grapefruit and a bowl of dried oatmeal that Richard had left out for him.

"I just bumped into a Mrs O'Dwyer? She said she knows a

124

Lew-wis?" I asked as I slipped watermelon pips from my mouth.

"Did you now," Abba said.

"Said that someone called Lewis got a bit tearful last night."

"Who did?"

"Mrs O'Dwyer, you know, that woman over there." I looked over at the O'Dwyers who were seated a few tables from us.

They waved.

"I don't think I was."

"Didn't you have dinner with them last night?"

Abba looked over his glasses. "Oh, yes, I think it was. Lovely people. What's their name again?"

"O'Dwyer. She said you got a bit upset and started crying."

"Maybe it was the pills and the wine."

"Nothing to do with the Holy Land then?" I laughed. "Hey Lewis, shall we go on pilgrimage to Bethlehem? What do you think?"

"Don't mock."

"I'm glad you made some friends."

"Friends? I wouldn't call them my friends. I don't have any friends."

"Well, you do now," I chuckled. "She said you told them some great stories."

"Well, at least someone finds me interesting."

"Why did she call you Lewis?" I asked.

"Because that's my name," Abba said, wiping his mouth with the back of his hand.

"No, it's not, it's Louis."

"I sometimes use Lewis with people I don't know, OK?"

"Don't you like your name?"

125

"Never have."

"What's wrong with it?"

"Lis-ten, I think it sounds a bit too Jewish. I used it when I was teaching in America and sometimes, it's useful. Is that OK with you?"

"But it's not your real name."

"I, just, don't, like it," he insisted and raised his hand, his signal that he wanted the conversation to end. "And by the way, I hated it when you used to call me Louis. What was wrong with Abba or daddy? It's all your mother's fault."

I sighed, knowing that here was something else he could blame my mother for. I don't know why I called him Louis rather than Abba throughout my teens. Maybe I thought it was more grown up, that he might pay me more attention.

"I'm not crazy about my name either you know," I said.

"There's nothing wrong with your name."

"Oh, apart from the fact that I was teased for years at school. 'Do you know where you can find Miki's pecker? Where? In his fucking name'… Ha, ha, ha. Doesn't even make sense. No one can spell or pronounce it anyway. Yeh, thanks for that."

"Balls! There's nothing wrong with your name. It's a great name."

A great name for who? This conversation wasn't going anywhere, and this wasn't on my list of questions, so I dropped it.

A breeze drifted across the pool as the sun scorched our sweating bodies. I knew I should pick up *Herzog* and struggle on. It lay on the ground staring up at me. I ran my eyes over a few pages, looking for hints and clues in the text of where it was going,

126

trying to catch a glimpse of what was next. But I quickly lost interest, and instead watched some children play in the kids' pool, screaming as water guns were fired at them every few seconds from different directions. I yearned to join them, keen for the blasts of water to pulsate my skin and throw me backwards.

My eyes followed Abba as he went to pee, criss-cross creases from the sun lounger indenting his back and legs. The hairs on his arms had turned blond in the sun, and his head was pink and raw. He'd hoisted his swimming shorts high above his waist, covering his hernia. Sometimes, he complained that it felt hot. Like an itchy broken limb under a cast, he'd reach under his clothes and give the firm, fatty growth a decent rub.

A pale scar travelled the length of Abba's calf on his right leg, leftover from his triple heart bypass. Embedded into the left side of his chest was a pacemaker that protruded squarely under his skin the size of a box of matches. I imagined the tiny wires sparking his heart on demand, intelligently reading the pace of his beat, like jump-start cables igniting rhythm and fixing murmurs. Deep purple bruises dotted the side of his right arm and leg from his fall in the restaurant and a trip a few weeks earlier on uneven paving stones outside Walshe's pharmacy in Dublin.

His body seemed lost, as if it had forgotten how to move, like an actor unsure of where to stand on stage. It amazed me that it still functioned, but also annoyed me that he'd allowed it to waste away so that it was now beyond repair. I'd always wanted a father who would be active with his son, like my friends' dads. Maybe we could play tennis? Perhaps father and son doubles. But all I got were repetitive stories of his triumphs and disappointments on the tennis court in his teens, and how a coach had changed and ruined his game. To my surprise, he agreed to play tennis with me one day on holiday when I was still at school. Drink in one hand, racquet in the other, he hit two forehands with worn balls that disappeared into overgrown bushes at the back of the court. I was dispatched to look for them, but they were lost. We didn't play again.

"I'm off for a snooze," Abba said, "it's too bloody hot."

Abba held my wrist as we walked back to the apartment where we retreated for some shade. He slept as I flicked channels on the television, looking for something to catch my attention, but I could only find the news in Spanish and mid-morning soaps.

"You there?" Abba shouted from his room a few hours later.

"Yeh," I mumbled, rubbing my eyes. I'd fallen asleep on the sofa.

"I need you. Quick."

"One sec..." I turned off the television.

"Now!"

"What's wrong?" I asked, standing next to his bed. His head was propped up on his pillows. He was breathing rapidly.

"I need to go in."

"What?"

"I've got to go in," he said again, hurriedly.

"Go in where?"

"Hospital. Get Steinberg to meet us there."

"What?"

"Get Steinberg for God's sake. I need to go. Now!"

"What's wrong?"

"I'm having a heart attack."

"What? Where?"

"Here," he said, pointing to his chest.

"Jesus! Really?" I held my hand over my mouth. I scrunched my eyes together. For a few moments I had no idea what to do. I ran out of his room to the hall of the apartment as if I wanted to get out. I stopped. Fuck. He can't be having a heart attack now. He was fine only a couple of hours before. I didn't know what to do. Abba always seemed to know what to do. Why didn't I know? Breathe, I said to myself. Breathe. Water. I'll get him some water. He'll be fine. Should I call my mother? Should I call Richard? Shit.

"What should I do?" I shouted as I filled a glass of water.

"Call a bloody ambulance!"

"Wait, wait!" I took a deep breath as I re-entered his room. "Are you sure it's not indigestion? It could be something you ate."

"I know what it feels like."

He stared at me.

"OK." I paused. "Why don't we call Steinberg and ask him to come here so he can see what the problem is. I'm sure it's nothing serious."

"There's no time, we have to go in!"

"OK, I'll… I'll ask Richard to call an ambulance. Don't worry, you'll be fine," I said, the glass of water now shaking in my hand. I wanted to hug him, but something held me back. Maybe I was afraid to catch what he had, so I lightly felt his forehead with the back of my hand. It was clammy and cold.

Five years earlier, I lay awake in my bed one morning, the ceiling spinning rapidly. My heart pulsated like a drum in my chest.

It echoed in my ears, my toes, the vein at the side of my head. My mouth was dry, my forehead ached, the muscles on the left of my chest were tight, my fingertips numb, my back cold, my palms sweaty.

I dialled an ex-girlfriend. No answer. I walked to the front door of my apartment. I checked my phone repeatedly. I scrubbed the dirty dishes. I walked to the front door. I took two Solpadeine. I showered in cold water. I smoked a cigarette. I walked to the front door. I couldn't read. I couldn't lie down. I couldn't sit still. I couldn't think. I floated as I moved. I tried to call Abba. He'd know what to do. No answer.

I took myself to hospital.

Within minutes I was lying on a stretcher and my t-shirt had been removed by a nurse. Electrode pads were stuck to my chest and back. A heart monitor was clipped onto my forefinger, and a machine printed graphs and numbers on slips of paper that curled out like a till receipt. *How did it come to this*? I thought, as I lay there, cold and alone for what seemed like hours.

"Don't worry, you're not having a heart attack," a softly-spoken doctor said. I flinched as she ripped off the pads. She sat down opposite me in the cubicle and examined the receipts. "You're perfectly healthy, but you have what we call tachycardia."

"What's that?" I asked.

"A fast heart rate that doesn't settle when resting."

"Can't I take something?"

"Here's a leaflet and some beta blockers which will slow your heart."

"Can I go back to work?"

"You need to go home and get some rest."

"But will it pass?" I asked.

"Do you suffer from anxiety?"

"No," I said, shaking my head, holding back tears.

"Do you have someone to talk to?" she asked as she signed my notes.

You. You. You seem nice. Can I talk to you? Will you hold my hand? I wanted to say, but just stared at her.

"Please, see your GP, OK?" she said with a serious tone.

Feeling strangely proud, I called Abba later that evening to tell him about my trip to the hospital. We talked for well over an hour about heart rates, test results and blood pressure. Finally, we had something in common. "Beta blockers will do the trick," he said approvingly, and prescribed plenty of walking, eating less red meat and some breathing exercises. "Relax," he said, "you've nothing to worry about. You'll be fine." I believed him.

Five minutes later Richard barged past me as I opened the door to our apartment. He was wearing a water polo skullcap with ear pads that made him look more like a Russian cosmonaut than a holiday rep. A worried looking Ines followed.

"The ambulance is on its way. Where is he?" Richard asked.

"In bed, lying down," I said.

"Is he, like, OK?"

"I'm not sure."

"What happened?"

"Said he's having a heart attack."

"A wha?"

"Heart attack."

131

"Jesus, that's never happened on my watch."

Ines covered Abba with a bobbly beige blanket we found in a cupboard. I wondered how many people had slept under the blanket, and how long it had been folded up gathering dust. Abba looked perfectly still, almost statute-like, his head poking out one end, his feet poking out the other.

I was six or seven years old when I woke to blue lights circling around my childhood bedroom in my parents' house in Dublin. I could hear voices, so got up and moved to the top of the stairs, my vantage point, my eagle's nest. From there I watched through the bannisters as men in green overalls looked over Abba who was lying at the bottom of the stairs, partially covered in the red blanket from my parents' bed. One man raised Abba's head and strapped an oxygen mask over his face, while his other hand pumped a large plastic tube. Another man held his hand on Abba's wrist, and every few seconds looked at his watch. Abba seemed unrecognisable to me, like a stranger who didn't belong in our house. "Let's go now," one of the men said. "Oh God," my mother cried when she saw me, running up the stairs and kissing my forehead with a smile. She told me not to be afraid, and that she'd be back, at some point. They lifted Abba onto a stretcher and wheeled him towards the blue lights, the gate of our front garden banging three times against the metal railing behind them. I wasn't allowed to see him for a few weeks after that; over sixteens only, but I always knew he'd come home.

The front gate to our house was cast-iron. It was like a gong announcing someone's arrival. As a child I'd listen carefully for the gate. The first sign of it creaking open was my signal to get ready for Abba's return home. It was critical to be ready. I had to act the moment I heard it opening. I'd only have three, maximum five seconds to react to whatever I was doing. By that time, the front door would be open, and the last thing I wanted was for him to catch me watching TV and say, "Turn that bloody rubbish off." Quickly, I'd jump from the sofa, turn off the television in the lounge with the switch, not the remote, as he'd know from the green light on the box that it was still on, and leap, three steps at a time up to my bedroom. It was like a game to me, and I'd give myself points for speed and accuracy of execution. In a way I looked forward to the challenge, and welcomed his return, as if he was testing me. He knew full well that I was watching television, but I also hoped that I'd impress him by not being caught in the act.

But at night, when the house was still and the only sounds were the late-night taxis and the shouts of revellers leaving the pub at the top of the road, I'd lie in bed longing for the bang of the gate. I'd strain my eyes reading, and play the same cassettes repeatedly just to stay awake. I'd count the dots on my wallpaper. Abba always came home. The gate always banged. It was always a relief. I didn't need to see him. I just needed to know that he was there.

"Abba," I said, stroking his cheek, "Richard called an ambulance, and Steinberg said he'll get to the hospital as soon as he can."

"Yes, Steinberg, get Steinberg," he appealed, and drifted off again.

As we waited for the ambulance to arrive, Ines sat next to

Abba and held his hand, her thumb running over the veins under his skin that bulged like tree roots. Eventually, two paramedics entered. Introducing themselves as Juan and Angel, they methodically listened to Abba's heart and breathing, took his pulse and blood pressure, and slowly roused him. Juan put his arm around my shoulder and whispered, "Don't worry, I think he's OK, but we'll take him to hospital just to be sure." My lungs opened.

"Mister," Juan said to Abba.

"Yep. Steinberg? Are we in?" Abba asked.

"No, they think you should go to hospital for some tests," I said.

"Right, let's go," Abba said excitedly.

Juan and Angel lifted Abba onto a stretcher and steered him out of the room. A crowd parted as we left the lift and entered the hotel lobby. The teenage girl I'd seen earlier with Joe was furiously texting, and the O'Dwyers both made the sign of the cross on their chests.

"Can I join you?" Richard asked me as we walked towards the waiting ambulance.

"What?" I said.

"I've never, like, been in an ambulance before, you know," he said, looking at me like an excited child.

Richard climbed into the back of the ambulance and closed the doors, his eyes fixated on the machines that beeped and blinked. The ambulance drove off, gently rolling from side to side over endless speed bumps. Abba remained still. Perhaps he was afraid to move until the feeling passed, like a scared animal dazzled by headlights hoping the crash wouldn't come. The windows were darkened. I had no idea where we were going, as if we were drifting through a kind of no man's land.

Abba never freely admitted it, but I knew that death frightened him. The obituaries were the first thing he'd read in *The Irish Times* every morning. He'd comment about television colleagues and old pals from the theatre he knew that had died, were about to die, or looked as if they were on their way out. Appointments to Beaumont, St James', St Vincent's, The Mater hospitals for blood tests, Warfarin checks, cardiology appointments, diabetes consultations and physiotherapy filled his week. And of course, he'd eagerly recount each visit to us like a diary entry.

Sometimes, he'd sit us down at the dinner table and announce that he believed his time was coming to an end, and that we should prepare. He made a rule; no going out on Friday nights. We shouldn't go away on holiday too often either, just in case it happened and we weren't at home. We had to put our lives on hold for him. But I always sensed that he was desperate to stay, just a little bit longer.

Now calm and alert, I knew that there wasn't much wrong with him, but I was on autopilot, I knew the drill. Any hint of feeling unwell and in he went, once again to the hospital.

Richard left us waiting in the Emergency Room of the Hospital Del Sur, which was crowded with crying babies, people coughing and sneezing and talking on mobile phones. I filled two cups of water and helped Abba take some sips as he lay on a stretcher, bare-chested, electrode pads strung up to a heart monitor. At some stage the curtains of a cubicle opposite us were opened like a play, showing a person writhing in pain, bloody bandages littered on the floor. We both tried to peep in, excited by the speed of movement of the doctors, the machines, needles and tubes, then looked away when the patient cried out. Every time a nurse or doctor came towards us, they walked straight past, leaving us in limbo to watch the show and wait.

A couple of hours later, Doctor Steinberg examined Abba in the Santa Maria ward. Eight wires fixed onto pads had been suctioned to his chest. A cannula inserted into his left wrist was attached to a drip, and a heart monitor clip clasped onto his forefinger.

"You see, I told you he'd come," Abba said looking up at me.

"Yes, I called him," I said.

"Mr Lentin, you have had a false alarm," said Steinberg. He was wearing scrubs and a stethoscope hung from his neck.

"Really?"

"There is in fact very little wrong with you. As far as I can see you have had a minor bout of indigestion and a little bit of angina, which is not uncommon for a man of your age."

I sighed and turned away.

"You see, I knew it was my ticker," Abba said.

"I'm happy to tell you that your heart is doing fine, but you are on far too many different drugs and there is too much alcohol in your system. Believe you me there are many other people on this island who are a lot worse off than you," said Steinberg.

"But I felt it in my arm, my chest. I've had attacks before you know, this isn't my first."

"Your son told me. When was your last heart attack?" Steinberg asked.

"Ten years ago? I can't remember exactly."

"And since then?"

"I have developed back ache, diabetes, type two that is, neuropathy in my feet, I need to pee a lot, and this bloody thing." Abba lifted his sheet and pointed to his hernia. "It's so damn hot."

"You mentioned all of this the last time we met. But considering your history and other ailments, your heart is in good shape. Is it too hot for you here?"

"Not at all, I adore the sun. That's why we came," Abba said. He smiled.

"You must be careful that you don't overheat, and you should drink a lot of water, and maybe a little less alcohol? It's very high in sugar."

"But I'm on holiday."

"Abba, listen to what he's telling you," I said.

"I like it," he said turning to me.

"Mr Lentin…"

"Please, call me Lewis."

"Mr Lentin," Steinberg breathed, "I suggest you stay here for the night, get some rest, cool down, and then we'll see if you can return to the hotel tomorrow. How many more days are you here?"

"Two," I said.

"So you have two days to recover, then you can fly home and see your doctor. The nurses will look after you now."

"Will you come back?" Abba looked up at Steinberg almost child-like.

"I've a lot of patients to see, today and tomorrow."

"I wanted to give you a copy of the Philip Roth book I told you about. I really think you'd enjoy it."

"As I said, I don't read much in English."

"But he makes everything so, so simple."

"I must go now," Steinberg said, fiddling with his pager.

"Maybe we'll come by your surgery tomorrow or the next day, and you can advise me on the drugs I'm taking. It would be marvellous to talk it through."

"Don't you think you should see your doctor at home?"

"He can't see his doctor anymore," I said.

"Oh, why?" Steinberg asked.

"You tell him," I said.

"No reason."

"Go on," I said.

"Please, don't upset him," Steinberg said. He raised his eyebrows at me. "This whole experience has put enough strain on his body, and he should try and get some sleep."

"I don't respect him, that's why," Abba said.

"Well, that's a matter for you and your doctor, but I would advise against me changing your prescriptions without a lot more information about your background and symptoms."

"Why don't you tell him the truth?" I asked Abba.

"The truth about what?"

"O'Neill."

"O'Neill? That..." Abba pursed his lips and looked up at the ceiling. "You know," he said, pointing his finger at me, "every time I went to see him, every time I made a bloody appointment he was on holiday. Every bloody time! He was never there when I needed him."

"Enjoy the rest of your holiday." Steinberg shook Abba's hand, and left the ward, his trainers squeaking down the corridor.

"Why didn't you just tell him that O'Neill threw you out?" I asked.

"Why don't you mind your own bloody business?"

"While we're here, you are my business. You have to stop wasting peoples' time."

"I'm not wasting anyone's time, apart from yours obviously."

"You are! You know there's not much wrong with you. Every time it's the same thing. Why are we even here? You could be outside, on the beach, enjoying the sun you love so much, but oh no, we're in a bloody hospital, again." I looked closely into his eyes. I looked and I looked. I didn't blink.

I turned towards the window, stared out over the car park and counted the cacti that had been planted in rows between the cars. In the distance, small pockets of smoke puffed from a tower behind a modern looking church. I spent a few minutes watching them as they evaporated into the late afternoon sky.

Abba had a triple bypass operation just after my *Bar Mitzvah*. One night, over dinner, he announced that he was having surgery. "It's nothing," he said, "the surgeon will take a cholesterol-clear vein from one of my legs and replace the blocked vein that goes into my heart with the clear one. They'll staple me up afterwards. I'll be fine." And of course, we were told in great detail about the surgeon, one of Ireland's best, who had done hundreds of these operations which were now popular among men in their mid-forties. Abba went through the plans and seemed pleased that he'd be "going in", as he liked to call it. The hospital, Blackrock Clinic, was private, and he'd have his own room, with a view. "From the brochure, it looks pleasant enough," he said. There'd be a glass of red wine on offer a few days after the "op", and we could visit, as often as we liked.

I sobbed when I saw Abba in intensive care a few days later. His chest, usually a jungle of grey hair had been shaved and split open and was now held together with thick staples. Blood saturated bandages were wrapped around his left leg that was held up on a pulley. Thinner and jaundiced, something made me not want to touch him, as if he was unclean. An itch ran over my skin, like I'd been bitten by tiny midges. My legs were restless. I wanted to run out of the claustrophobic, antiseptic smelling room, down the corridor and into the fresh air.

As the weeks went by and Abba began to recover, he told us stories about how great the hospital was. The food. Fish pie one day. Steak the other. The glass of red wine he was allowed with dinner. The books he could read and music he listened to. All in peace and quiet. He'd set up a home away from home, as if he'd retreated into a space of complete belonging where he knew he'd get the constant attention he craved. No brown rice, which my mother had taken to cooking, no one to disagree with him about Israel, and no football watching.

My mother, sister and I would visit every couple of days. I'd grumpily get out of the car, Walkman headphones on, and look up at his room that was visible from the car park. From there I could just about make him out, sitting contentedly at a coffee table by the window, reading or eating alone in his dressing gown and furry slippers. Once in his room, I never kissed or hugged him and stayed in the corner, my leg twitching while he gave us all an update on how he was doing, what he'd had for dinner, what opera he'd listened to that day, who had returned from surgery, who was recovering, who had died.

My teachers and friends' parents had seen a front-page article in *The Irish Times* about Abba's operation and often asked me how he was, but I just shrugged, indifferent to their questions. Why didn't anyone ask me how I was feeling or how my mother was? What would they say if I told them what I really felt?

A boy in my class lost his father that same year, and every morning for a few months during *Shacharit*, morning prayers at school, we accompanied him in singing *Kaddish*, the mourner's prayer. The boy seemed petrified at first. Pale, he didn't eat or drink. He sat alone and scratched himself. He didn't play with anyone. He was teased for leaving the door of the bathroom open when he sat on the toilet. He got off doing his homework. He was collected early by his mother every day. But after a few months, the colour returned to his face, he started playing football again. He hung around with his friends at playtime. He became the teacher's pet, as if nothing much had happened. It didn't seem that bad. I'd be able to cope.

While he lapped up the luxury of Blackrock, Abba once again became a stranger to me, so perhaps it wasn't surprising that at times I didn't want him to survive his recovery. I often wondered if we'd be better off if he wasn't around. Without Abba's domineering presence at home, our family life became easier. We ate in the kitchen rather than the dining room. I didn't have to worry about turning off the television whenever he came home. We didn't have to talk about Israel every night. I knew I missed him but wasn't sure how.

After one final glass of wine and a last supper of lobster, Abba returned home from Blackrock Clinic. He informed us that carrying heavy bags would put too much strain on his heart, he had to eat nutritiously, walk regularly and not get into stressful situations. He did it for a few weeks and I hoped that over time things might change, but nothing really did. He continued to drink, and when he fought with my mother or things became stressful at work, he attempted to re-create the experience of being in the private clinic by retreating to the sanctuary of his bedroom. There, he'd just lie awake on the bed, staring into space, or read, often for hours alone, the door always ajar. Maybe he was waiting for something to happen, to hear what else was going on in his absence, but he wasn't to be disturbed.

As I arrived back at Abba's ward later that evening, I walked past hospital attendants in plastic aprons serving food from steaming pots. The bright overhead lights reflected against the windows, making everything outside resemble a sea of black. Most of the other beds were unoccupied, apart from one, where an elderly man repeated the commentary from a football match he was watching loudly on TV.

"Abba, I brought you some things," I said, as the curtain surrounding his bed rattled open. His eyes were closed, so I quietly tidied away his dressing gown, worn toothbrush, *The World of Yesterday*, wash bag and a bottle of water. The armchair next to his bed looked inviting. My body fell into it, easing the tension of the day. The heart monitor beeped regularly. It read seventy-two beats per minute. He was fine.

"*Señor, hora de la cena, despierta*," a hospital attendant said, as she pushed a trolley laden with pots of food into the ward.

"Abba, there's some dinner here if you want it," I said. I shook

142

him gently.

Abba stretched as he stirred. I helped him sit up, plumped his pillows and lifted the back of his bed to a seated position.

"Looks good," I said, removing the plastic lid.

"What's on offer?"

"Pasta, salad and cheese."

"Let's hope it's better than what I get at home. *Yesh ya'in*, is there wine?" Abba asked.

"Now?"

"Why not? It's good for the heart."

"Here, have some water."

I flicked through *The World of Yesterday* as Abba finished every morsel.

"Marvellous," he said, wiping his mouth with a paper towel, "I think I'll make some notes for the next time I go in at home. Suggest a few improvements." He smiled.

"You do that," I said forlornly, and cleared away his dinner tray.

"Why do you take everything I say so seriously?"

I ignored him. I wanted to ask him why he enjoyed hospitals so much. What was it about them that injected him with so much life when most people found them depressing? But after a long day I didn't feel like starting with my questions. The air conditioning had sucked me dry, and I was keen to get back to the hotel to wash away the disinfectant that filled my lungs like a thick layer of cellophane.

"I'm off," I said.

"So soon?"

"I wouldn't mind an early night."

"OK maestro. Thanks, you know, for everything."

"I'll see you in the morning. Sleep well." I kissed his forehead.

"God bless." He smiled, holding onto my hand for a moment, before opening his book.

The hospital was quietening down for the night. As I walked towards the exit, I looked into rooms that had been occupied earlier in the day that were now empty, beds made, belongings taken home, flowers and cards disposed of. I told myself there was nothing wrong with Abba, but every time I left him alone in hospital the same momentary feeling that I'd forgotten something would hang over me. As I walked out into the cool night air, I knew he'd still be there when I collected him the next morning. He always was.

"How's your dad?" Richard asked, as I sat on a worn banquette in the hotel bar staring into a whiskey.

"Fine. I'll collect him in the morning," I said.

"He had me worried there for a while, you know."

"And me."

"You know, I know what it's like," Richard said.

"What do you mean?"

"My mum, she died a few years ago." Richard's eyes moistened.

"Sorry to hear that."

"Cancer. Fucking killed her. Just killed her life you know. Ruined it. She had to live with it for years. Like a curse it was. She was always in pain. In and out of hospital for this treatment and that procedure, every day, even when the doctors said that she was more or less OK and could live a normal life. It kind of took over, as if she couldn't give it up. Drove my dad and my sisters mad. That's why I left, to get away from it. Your dad reminds me of her. Stubborn she was. Stubborn as anything. Always her way," he laughed, "always her fucking way…"

"That must have been difficult."

"She's better off where she is now, wherever that is. Do you believe in God?"

"I'm not sure."

"She did. Oh, she really did."

"What about you?"

"I'm like you, I don't know. It's just a good story I suppose. People can believe what they want to believe. I'm OK with that. At least that's what I think." He paused. "Can I get you another?"

"Sure."

I found the folded piece of paper in my wallet and twisted it around my fingers. With only two days left, the chances of asking Abba my questions were fading fast. He'd be tired tomorrow, probably sleep most of the day. And anyway, why should I subject an old, ill, frail man to my selfish problems? Maybe I just had to let things go and move on. The alcohol made me sleepy as I listened to the piano-man in a white tuxedo play soppy eighties' tracks on the hotel piano. I watched a couple slow dance across the wooden floor under a few flashing spotlights. The banquette accepted me as I lay down. It felt good to curl up, rest my head on my arms and caress my knees into my chest. The couple blurred into one as the whiskey danced in my head, and slowly I fell asleep.

…As for telling me about your feelings, I can't tell you how thrilled and happy I am for you! At your age, or indeed any age it's so wonderful to find someone special. But perhaps I should have explained to you before that there are at least two rules to be observed when taking young ladies (or otherwise) to balls, hops or similar events… a/ never take two, half a dozen if you must indulge yourself, then you can have a ball, but two? Where's the fun in two, both of whom wish to tear you in half, and b/ if you must give them flowers and very generous you were too, and thoughtful as is your want, for God's sake do not give them funeral wreaths. It's difficult enough to dance to some of those modern hokey pokeys where all you seem to do is rap each other, but to expect your half-partners to do that with wreaths around their necks is asking for trouble. No wonder one went home early and the other wouldn't talk to you. I can't say I blame them…

DAY EIGHT

The Last Supper

Richard had recommended that we try La Bella Luna, a restaurant in La Caleta for our last supper. He said it was romantic. Just what Abba and I needed. Abba was initially reluctant to go with "that Fella's" suggestion, despite Richard's help the day before, and I detected a hint of disappointment that I hadn't planned a return to Steinberg's favourite restaurant. But, he said "it would do" as long as they served pleasant, authentic, local food with decent wine. I wasn't bothered where we ate. It was our last night. His overnight stay in hospital had exhausted him. I wanted him to go home happy. I was ready to go home.

La Bella Luna was perched at the end of a beach next to a fishing harbour. Faded murals of fishermen in flat caps and jumpers adorned the walls, and fairy lights cascaded down wooden pillars. I could hear the distant sound of rigging flapping in the wind.

Abba marched into the restaurant towards an empty table by the back wall.

"*Señor!*" a waiter called after him.

"What's wrong with that one?" Abba asked pointing to an unoccupied table.

"It's reserved," the waiter said.

"It looks free to me."

"Please." The waiter pulled out two chairs from a table in the centre of the restaurant.

"You should never have trusted that fella," Abba sighed.

I didn't understand why it mattered where we sat in restaurants. I always grabbed the first table I could find. Surely they were all the same? Abba though, insisted on choosing a table closest to the wall. Dining out was like theatre to him. He had to have an unobstructed view of what was playing out in front of him, the best seat in the house.

We sat on wicker chairs with thin cushions. A tea light flickered in the breeze and a single rose in a jug rested in the centre of the table. I wriggled uncomfortably in my seat and jiggled my legs. A metallic taste from lunch that I couldn't get rid of filled my mouth. Everything itched.

"I'm going to wash my hands," I said.

Abba didn't look up from the laminated menu.

The cream-tiled cubicle was narrow and stank of potpourri. I removed my wallet from the back pocket of my jeans, and hoping I hadn't lost it, searched for the piece of paper with my list of questions. It was there.

It had been a few months since I'd scribbled onto this piece of paper in my shrink's living room. She'd suggested it would be helpful.

My hands shook, nervous to unfold it, as if I was about to get some exam results. My breath was shallow. I felt tight. Resting two fingers on my wrist, I watched the second hand of my watch turn as I timed my speeding heart. I thought of chucking months of angst and memories down the toilet, but quickly unfolded the paper and read it to myself:

149

Friday, September 7, 2006, London

Dear Abba,

I'm writing this to you from the house of my therapist. Rather than talk today, she thought it would be a good idea to jot down a few questions, things I've always wanted to know, but have never had a chance to ask or discuss with you. Here goes...

Why didn't you want to do things with me that I was interested in?
Did you care that I didn't like you shouting and arguing all the time?
Why did you just leave Israel that time without saying goodbye?
Why didn't you look after yourself properly?
What changed? Sometimes you were happy and other times you seemed so unhappy. Why?

I know you'll say that I'm over-reacting and that these things happen and that we always accuse you of this or that, and why am I dwelling on the past? But they are important to me, so maybe we'll get to discuss them, one day.

With love,
Your son.

As I finished reading the bathroom light clicked off. Sitting in pitch black, I waved my arms, hoping a sensor would turn it back on. It didn't. I felt the wall, searching for the light switch but couldn't find it. Shit. I heard the distant shouts of chefs and the banging of pans from the kitchen. Someone tried to open the door. "Just a minute," I muttered. Feeling in front of me I found the door handle and key. I shook it from side to side but it wouldn't turn. I yanked it out of the lock but dropped it as I tried to shove it back in to place. I scrambled on the ground for the key, my hands slipping on water blown from the hand dryer, eventually finding it by the door frame. A loud knock made me jump. The hand dryer whooshed on, blasting my head with hot air. I felt my way back to the toilet seat and sat back down. Should I bang on the door for help? Who would look after Abba? Would someone rescue me, or would I be found a few hours later, stinking of potpourri, still gripping my questions? Feeling the key in my hand, I guided it gently back into the lock with my fingers and turned. It clicked, unlocking and opening the door. The light stung my eyes as it came back on. I threw some water onto my face, and feeling refreshed, walked back to our table. I was ready.

Abba looked smart and clean. While he'd slept by the pool in the afternoon sun earlier that day, I did some laundry, as if I'd wanted to wash away the memories of the holiday before it had ended. He was wearing a pair of ironed khaki chinos, a short-sleeved pink and white striped shirt, socks and sandals. His ever-present smock hung from his shoulders, like an adult comfort blanket. Dark rings drooped like horseshoes under his eyes. His face was singed pink. Usually he looked forward to a good meal, but tonight he seemed distant, like he'd just woken from a deep sleep. He slouched forward over the edge of the table, his head resting in one hand, while the other rubbed his hernia.

"How is it?" I asked.

"Hot, like my bloody feet," Abba said.

"Hasn't the sun helped?"

"A bit."

He yawned and stretched his arms out to the side, as if he didn't quite know what to do with them.

"Tired?" I asked.

"I just need a drink."

"Remember what Steinberg said."

"Ah come on, it's my last night."

"You should listen to his advice you know."

"What's taking them?" Abba asked while looking around. A waiter sauntered over and placed a basket of crusty bread on the table.

"It's Friday night, shall we do *Shabbat*?" I asked, realising we'd been away for a week.

"If you insist."

"I thought you enjoyed it."

"It just doesn't seem right here."

"Why not?"

"I wouldn't mind so much if we were sitting over there. And there's a bloody draft," he said, rubbing the back of his neck.

I clenched my fists under the table, willing him to enjoy himself, but tonight he looked as if he'd given up. "Do you remember," I chuckled, "you insisted that we sang Kiddush every Friday night, even when we had non-Jewish guests over."

"It was the right thing to do."

"But it was so embarrassing."

"I wasn't embarrassed."

I'd stand with my hands in my pockets and stare out of the

window of our dining room as Abba conducted my mother, my sister and me like a choirmaster. Our guests smiled or hummed along, as they looked down at their feet, unsure if they had to stand or sit as we chanted.

"Why are you so self-conscious all of a sudden?" he asked.

"You're the one who's being self-conscious. It's just funny, thinking about it now." I paused. "Shall we?"

"You do it, I'll conduct."

I blessed the tea light quietly, my hands cupped around its edges. Then, holding up my glass of water, I sang the prayer for the wine and passed it to Abba who sipped a bit. Feeling alone, I blessed the bread to myself rather than with Abba, and started to sing *Shalom Aleichem*, a *Shabbat* song, as the loud chatter and laughter from other tables filled my ears. I looked around to see if anyone was watching. Couples stared into each other's eyes, some holding hands, others silent, while larger tables were packed with people who were too busy grabbing drumsticks, prawns and fillets of fish from silver platters to pay any attention to us. At first, the low notes of the song got stuck in the back of my throat, as if I'd forgotten the words, but as the tune developed, the notes began to vibrate into my bones, my jaw, my fingers. I decided to sing the long version. Maybe he'd join in, and we'd sing together, like two tenors. After a few verses he started to conduct, raising his arm up and down like a metronome with a hint of a smile, but he quickly flopped it down. My notes flatly petered out. I tore at the bread, sprinkled it with salt, and passed a piece to Abba. We chewed, and using our fingertips, picked at the salty crumbs that fell onto the table.

"My name is Miguel. I will be your waiter tonight," the waiter said. He was wearing black trousers and a black waistcoat over a white shirt with a frayed collar. His hair was slick with oil and his teeth were surprisingly white, as if they'd been bleached.

"I hate these Americanisms," Abba mumbled. "Well, my name is Lewis, and this is my son."

I rolled my eyes.

"*Mucho gusto.* Are you ready?" Miguel asked.

"Lobster!" Abba announced, sitting up straight in his chair.

"I thought you said on the way that you fancied a steak?" I said.

"I changed my mind. I'm allowed to do that. Is it fresh?"

"Fresh? My uncle's the fisherman," Miguel said.

"Must be the same uncle who gets the fish for the other place," Abba laughed.

"Abba..." I mouthed while staring at him.

"And you're certain it's not frozen?"

"*Señor*, please. To drink?"

"Champagna?" Abba asked.

"Tenerife champagne is excellent," Miguel said.

"Great, a bottle please Miguel. It's my last night. I'd like to enjoy myself."

"*L'Chaim*, cheers," I said, as we clinked glasses that Miguel had filled with champagne.

"*L'Chaim*," Abba said. "Lis-ten, sorry about all that fuss yesterday. I'm not sure what happened. I feel much better now. I've had a great time. Thanks for coming. You're a great man. A solid man."

He often called me "great" and "solid", even though I had no idea what he meant. I didn't ever feel great or solid, at least not at that moment. Abba briefly raised his eyes to me as if he had something else to say but didn't. Instead, he concentrated on steadying his shaking hands as he sipped his champagne.

"I thought I'd start the Bashevis-Singer on the plane," Abba said.

"You done with Zweig?" I asked, as the bubbles from the champagne fizzed the back of my throat.

"Finished it today. I haven't read *The Slave* in years."

"What's it about?"

"From what I can remember, it's about this Polish slave, who happens to be Jewish. He works as a shepherd and low and behold, falls in love with his Master's daughter, a *Shikse*."

"You mean a non-Jewish woman."

"A *Shikse*. Yes, a *Shikse*. Such an unpleasant word. Happened to me once you know."

Another story I'd heard many times.

"We met at university, and, for a few months I suppose… we were in love," he said. "We adored the theatre. She played, I directed." He closed his eyes. "We'd get the tram into town and go for a meal and a show, all for two and six pence. Sometimes we'd pop into Bewley's café on Grafton Street for a coffee and a sticky bun. It's not like it is today. There were these wonderful old women who served at tables, and you could smell the coffee from outside. None of this ordering at the counter nonsense. I'd take the old man's Austin and we'd drive to Dun Laoghaire and walk along the pier. I don't know what I was thinking." He shook his head. "Stupidly, stupidly I introduced her to my parents. So bloody stupid." He paused. "Next thing I know I was told to stop the whole damn thing. Get rid of her, they told me. They ganged up on me. The lot of them. Everyone always ganged up

155

on me. My father, my mother, my uncle, everyone. Why the hell did they care?"

"You could have run away, you might have been happy."

"That's what it was like back then. You know that. There was no way I would have been allowed to marry a *Shikse*. That was it. I had no option but do as I was told." He jabbed the table as he spoke.

I was never sure if he really had no option, or that was just what he told himself.

"But you might have been happy."

"You know, the funny thing is, I don't remember how she took it. Maybe I just explained, and that was that. Knowing her though, she probably fumed," he laughed. "*Shikse*, they called her. *Shikse*. Such a horrible word."

"But you might have been happy," I said louder.

"They never called her by her real name. Bastards, the lot of them. I was an embarrassment to the family, that's what they said. But I loved her, not that that was important to them," he said, wiping his moist eyes.

"And Imma, don't you love her?"

"Of course I do. I'm talking about the past. This happened years ago. It doesn't mean I'm not allowed to think about what could have been."

"Such as?"

Abba took a sip of his drink and leant in closer to me. "I've been thinking. Maybe I should have been with more women you know…"

This was a new one.

"Don't you ever think about it?"

"No!"

"Why not? Maybe, I could have, you know." He raised his eyebrows.

"Is that really what you really wanted?"

"Well it would have made things interesting," he laughed.

"But would you have been happy?"

"I heard you the first time you know."

"And?"

He shrugged. "I need to pee."

Abba grabbed on to the backs of chairs of other customers for support as he shuffled slowly towards the bathroom. Some of them glanced at him as he passed, shaken by the sudden jolt. He didn't stop to apologise.

My polyester cardigan felt stiff and itched my wrists. I ran my hands over the glass surface of the table and enjoyed the heat of the melted wax on my fingers as I picked at the tea light. Like an interval at the theatre, I hadn't worked out what would come next. There were too many thoughts in my mind, like scribbles in pencil on a piece of paper that are rubbed away, leaving eraser shavings scattered across the page. I waved the piece of paper with my questions over the flame of the tea light, but something held me back. I needed to try, one more time.

Miguel served two blistering orange lobsters on oval dinner plates, separate bowls of chips, *Papas Arrugadas* with red and green mojo sauces, and a green salad. Abba tucked a napkin into the top button of his shirt. He found the stainless steel lobster pliers difficult to hold, so I rolled up the sleeves of my shirt and stretched over the table to help him. The pliers kept slipping from my grasp, so I got up, and stood behind him. Putting my hands over his, we worked in tandem, like two workmen, crunching the shells of the lobster's body and claws with satisfying cracks. There was something animal-like about the experience of ripping a dead crustacean apart for our pleasure.

I sat down. Sweating with anticipation, we dug into the carcasses, picking out the sweet flesh that we smothered with garlic butter, licking our fingers clean and drying them on paper napkins that disintegrated in our hands. As we ate, the lights dimmed and the background music was turned up. I noticed a trio setting up in the corner of the restaurant, tuning a guitar, and lightly patting a set of hand-held drums.

Please don't come our way, please. He hates live music in restaurants.

"Ah Miguel," Abba said, grabbing the waiter as he walked past. "Any chance you can turn it down a bit?"

"You don't like the music?"

"Not particularly. What is it anyway?"

"Canta Canarias."

"Well turn it down a bit, will you?" Abba palmed his hand downwards.

Miguel blew his lips together and motioned to another waiter behind the bar to drop the volume.

Abba returned to sucking the lobster claws, digging his tongue into every crevice in search of any remaining morsels of flesh.

"Maspik, enough," Abba announced, removing the napkin from his chest and throwing it on to the table.

"Another bottle?" I asked.

"Pausa." Abba held up his hand.

Our plates were now strewn with broken and empty lobster shells. Abba sank back into his seat, dropped his shoulders and rested his hands on his lap. He'd stopped itching his hernia, and looked content for the first time that evening, like he was listening to a piece of classical music at home. Most evenings after dinner he'd remove a disc from its sleeve, and holding it by its edge without touching the grooves, place it on his Linn Sondek gramophone. He'd dim the lights, lie on the sofa, a drink in his hand, close his eyes, and listen as loudly as possible to the great symphonies, concertos and operas. "Join me," he'd sometimes suggest. I'd reluctantly agree to sit next to him and hold his hand, his eyelids gently flickering, as if he was being transported to another world. But this was his space, his time, and after a while our hands would separate, a signal that he wanted to be left alone. I'd tip-toe away, shut the door to the front room and leave him in his cocoon.

I was tempted to go outside for a cigarette. I'm not sure if he would have noticed. He might have realised after a while that I was gone, but for a short time, he'd probably sit quietly, in his own thoughts, order a drink and wait, knowing that I'd eventually return. But all I could think of was my shrink saying, "Ask him. Get out your questions. Show it to him. Read it out loud. Tell him what you feel." She expected me to report back on my return, and even though I was reluctant to disturb his moment of happiness, now seemed like a good time.

The live music rose in tempo from the other side of the restaurant. Abba ordered a brandy and a whiskey for me.

"Did you enjoy it?" I asked.

"Good choice maestro."

I fidgeted uncomfortably in my seat. "Richard told me this would be a quiet place to talk."

"I told you not to trust that Fella."

"Well he was very helpful yesterday."

"What did you want to talk about?"

"Eh… she told me, you know, that I should talk to you, ask you some questions," I blurted.

"Who are we talking about now?"

"My therapist."

"I've told you about my one, haven't I? Marvellous woman. Such a shame she's retiring. Mind you, not seeing her will save me a few euros."

"Is that all you're interested in?"

"Not at all, but frankly I'd be better off spending the money on a good meal. I wasn't getting much out of it anyway. Lis-ten if it's about that time in Aran, I—"

"This isn't about Aran," I interrupted. "There are some things I need to know."

"Sure there's always things I need to know," he laughed.

"This isn't about you."

"Oh?" Abba yawned as he stretched his arms wide again. "Come on, let's not argue, let's enjoy this," he said. "There'll be plenty of time to talk on the plane tomorrow."

"I don't want to talk tomorrow." There was no way we'd be able to talk squashed on the plane between people buying scratch cards and duty free. "It's never a good time is it? There's always something else…"

"No there isn't."

"There is, and you know it."

"Look, I'm sorry if my life doesn't run by your timetable. I'm tired, for God's sake."

"Well you know what? So am I."

"Ah give me a break, will you?"

His dismissal, even at that point, stung. I was to give him a break. That was it. It wasn't important what I thought. It wasn't important what I wanted to talk about. It wasn't worthy of conversation. It wasn't his fact. It wasn't his story. It wasn't him. That was that. That's all there was to say. He was tired. He needed a break. He should be left alone. I should leave him. Alone. End of. End. Of. So, I sat. Quietly. As I always did. And spent a few minutes picking bits of lobster from my teeth with a toothpick, shoving it into the gaps of my gums until they started to bleed.

Around the time I started seeing my shrink, I visited Abba and my mother in Dublin. We spent an afternoon visiting an exhibition of sculpture at an art gallery on St Stephen's Green he had been keen to see. The display, while impressive in scale, lacked subtlety. My mother and Abba had got into a heated discussion about the art and its meaning, or lack of meaning. Under the heat of the gallery spotlights, he launched into a tirade, as if the disagreement was a personal attack against him. He remonstrated with my mother, chastising her, using one of his harshest phrases, "for an intelligent woman, you really say the stupidest things."

Something snapped in me. I went for him. What right did he have to be so bloody rude? Why was he behaving this way? Abba was shocked by my response. Where was the quiet diplomat who stayed silent on the side-lines and watched the performance play out in front of him? Even my mother looked alarmed, her eyes telling me to calm down, it doesn't matter, we know what he's like.

As we left the gallery, Abba said he wanted to "have a word." I felt like a child again. We walked past flower beds uprooted for winter, autumn leaves that crunched under our feet and busts of Yeats and Joyce in St Stephen's Green. We sat at either end of a park bench. We didn't speak for a few minutes. It felt like hours.

"You never understand me," Abba talked through his hands. He didn't make eye contact, but spoke to the park, an invisible audience. "No one does."

"Why do you have to talk to Imma that way?"

"It was a discussion."

"Some discussion."

"What do you want from me?"

"I don't understand why you have to behave that way?"

A man stopped next to our bench and threw chunks of bread to the ducks in the nearby pond. A few eagerly hopped onto the bank and gathered at our feet as the bread was scattered, pecking each other as they fought over the food.

"I've spent years trying to work it out," Abba said as he kicked out at the ducks in front of him.

"Well, try harder!"

"Thanks a lot."

"For what?"

"For your support. All I ask is for some bloody support."

"You'll have my support when you admit that you shouldn't have been so rude. Admit it!" It was the first time I'd ever raised my voice at him.

Abba pinched his eyelids under his glasses. "OK, I'm sorry.

I seem to spend my whole life apologising."

The sky darkened and thick clouds swept over the park. Trees rustled in the wind, and gusts scattered the leaves. Both of us looked out onto the emptying green. Even though I knew he was wrong, why did I feel guilty for telling him how I felt? I had been truthful to him about my feelings so few times in my life, yet I was left empty and afraid, as if I should be the one to apologise. The next day I was leaving Dublin, and I knew I wouldn't see him for a few months. I worried that it could be the last time I'd see him alive, as by then his body was struggling to keep up with his intellect. I didn't apologise though, and after sitting in the cold for a few minutes we did up our coats and walked home.

Abba went to pee, returning after a few minutes. I wasn't sure if I could look at him.

"You know," Abba started up, "when I was younger, my parents never once hugged or kissed me. Not once. At least not that I can remember. It's just not what they did. They left me alone and I left them alone. I lived upstairs, they lived downstairs. We ate together, I played golf with the old man up at Edmondstown, bloody awful place, and that was it. Suited me fine. I wasn't angry with them at the time, but at some point I changed, I think. Something changed in me. I'm not sure when it happened."

"What changed do you think?"

Finally.

"I don't know." He shook his head. "Who are you? My therapist?"

"I want to understand."

"What do you want to understand?"

"Why you changed? What happened?"

"I don't know. I told you. I don't know."

I took a long gulp of my whiskey.

"You always do this," I said.

"Do what?"

"Make out that it's some kind of joke or that you don't know, when I think you do. You're the one who brought it up. You always do this," I continued. "I didn't ask you to tell me about your parents and your lack of hugs. For God's sake, that was more than sixty years ago. I didn't ask you to bring up your therapist. I didn't ask you to talk about the *Shikse*. I didn't ask you to talk about Israel all the bloody time. You always bring up the same things."

"I don't have anyone else to talk to. Your mother won't talk to me. And anyway, I thought you wanted to talk, so I'm talking." Yes, he was talking.

"I do, but you always stop before we've properly started."

"Really?"

"You do," I implored.

Miguel suddenly appeared. His teeth, his fucking teeth. "*Señores*, dessert?"

I shook my head as I stared at him. He walked away sheepishly.

"This," I said. I fumbled for my wallet, pulled out my piece of paper and waved it in front of Abba. "This is why I really came away with you. I wanted to ask you all of this. I'm not even sure what it says anymore. It's just questions on a piece of paper that mean something to me, but nothing to you, and now I don't even know where to start, because you're incapable of having a normal conversation." My face was flushed. My heart pounded in my searing ears.

"Here, let me see that," Abba said, flailing his hand at the paper, trying to grab it, nearly knocking over his drink.

I pulled it away from him. "I've carried it around all week, and thought I'd give it to you tonight and we could look at it together, and maybe we could go through each question, one by one."

"I'm on holiday for God's sake. I didn't come here to be interrogated."

"Nobody's interrogating you..."

"You are!"

"I'm not!" I reached into my cardigan pocket and took out my cigarettes. I quickly lit one from the tea light with shaky hands, burning out the wick that flooded with wax. "Not everything has to be a bloody argument. I just want to talk to you, like normal people do." I exhaled a long stream of smoke. "Do you remember anything, anything at all if it's not about you? I want to know about things between you and me, not you and you."

"What are you going to accuse me of now?"

"OK. How about when you saw me or didn't see me get knocked off my bike and you just walked past, as if I wasn't your son."

"I did not!"

"I remember it like it was yesterday. You saw the whole damn thing. I had to brake suddenly because some bloody car was pulling out of a driveway near the house and I ended up somersaulting over the handlebars. You were walking on the other side of the road. You must have seen me fall off. I was winded, my head was spinning, there was grit, blood and snot on my face and I was lying on the ground. I cried out to you,

165

'Abba, Abba,' but you just continued to walk, as if I was invisible, as if I was someone else's problem. You didn't even turn to look at me. Why did you ignore me? I called out to you. I needed you." A few other customers looked over as I raised my voice.

"Honestly I don't remember. How many years ago was this?"

"It doesn't matter. I still think about it."

"Just like I still think about my parents."

I took a long drag of my cigarette, the glow crisply burning the tobacco and paper. "You know... we only ever wanted you to be happy, but it was so difficult. Nothing pleased you. Nothing was good enough. Even this, tonight, I wanted you to enjoy it."

"I am enjoying it."

"But the table isn't right, the music is too loud, the draft. Nothing is ever good enough for you." I paused, as hot salty tears of relief cascaded down my sunburnt cheeks.

"It is good enough," he whispered.

"Well if that's the case, then fucking show it!"

As I cried, I hoped that at some stage he might get up and ruffle my hair with his hand like he did when I was a kid. Sometimes when departing the scene of yet another dinner time argument with my mother, he'd walk behind me and run his hand through my hair. I longed so much for that quick shot of comfort. The warmth of that ruffle lingered in me for hours. Whenever he did it, I felt like I was his son, part of him, that he truly loved me, and wasn't angry with me. But so often he'd just walk past and leave me waiting, my body screaming inside for his affection. Sometimes I'd become jumpy in anticipation of the ruffle and want it so badly that I'd long to chase after him and make him do it. I wanted to grab his hand, attach it to my

166

head and leave it there permanently, so that I wouldn't have to wait each time he rose from the dinner table, hoping, needing it to happen again. He didn't do it this time either.

"You can talk to me about anything," Abba said.

"Really?"

"Why the hell not?"

"Because you've never said that before."

"Well, there you are, I'm saying it now."

Abba handed me his handkerchief so I could blow my nose, the cloth's familiar softness and laundered smell comforting me.

"I'm sorry," I said. "I didn't mean to get upset."

"That's OK. I'm sorry too," he paused. "They won't do your heart any favours by the way." He pointed at the box of cigarettes. "And don't think I can't smell it off you every morning."

I didn't care, and flicked the ash into an empty lobster shell, watching the grey dust float in the leftover greasy butter.

An elderly man holding a twelve-string Spanish guitar and a younger man with an accordion started playing next to us. A woman with emerald studded earrings joined the two musicians and started to sing what sounded like an old melody, her words rhythmically filling the gaps between the beats of the music. She stood remarkably still as she sang, as if the ground was strengthening her voice. I didn't understand the lyrics, but the music had a solemn richness to it, a folky earthiness. Even though we didn't know the tune, Abba and I both started to hum along at the same time. As we did, the singer came closer to our table and, looking at us with a serious expression, conducted us through the rest of the song, three beats up, three beats down, her voice like an evening breeze piercing and resting my heart, before she brought her fingers together to signify its end.

Miguel tentatively returned with two dessert menus and scraped the lobster carcasses onto one plate. He'd probably seen it all before, families and couples bickering after a week pickling in the sun. As he tidied up, I scrunched up my piece of paper into a ball and threw it onto the detritus. I watched it for as long as I could after Miguel piled our dishes onto one arm and carried everything away, the kitchen door swinging behind him.

"*Arehucas.* On the house," Miguel said, arriving back at our table.

"What's this?" I asked.

"Tenerife rum. Dessert, coffee my friends?"

"Nothing for me," I said.

"Fancy sharing a tiramisu?" Abba asked.

We looked at each other and laughed.

"You know," Abba said.

"What?"

"Try not to make the same mistakes as me."

We sat for a while finishing off the creamy alcoholic dessert, our spoons clashing in the glass bowl. Abba knocked back his shot of Arehucas. His face was drained of colour, his eyes bloodshot and sleepy. As the breeze cooled, the musicians packed away their instruments, customers paid bills, finished glasses of wine and pushed their chairs under tables. One of a few tables left, Miguel circled us and every so often re-filled our water glasses. I got up to pay. Something was missing from my wallet. Maybe, I thought, it didn't really matter anymore.

…Sorry I'm such a lousy letter writer. Long chat with the mother this evening. She appears delighted with all of her inter-views so far and has yet to see any friends, although I dare say the income at Telecom Israel has gone up considerably. I'm fed up being on my own and miss your mother and you more than I can tell you…

Alone

I dumped our used duvet covers, sheets and towels into a pile in the bathroom. The apartment that had been our home for eight days was now empty of our belongings. As I checked to see if we'd left anything behind, Abba sat still on the balcony, almost sculpture-like, possibly eager to catch a few final rays. The bright morning sun cast his shadow onto a wall. His eyelids twitched. His mouth was closed. Stray hairs curled from his scalp. Every so often he'd lick his lips and rub the back of his neck to ease the prickliness of the heat.

I was surprised to find that Abba had left his cherished dressing gown hanging on the back of his bedroom door. Digging into the pockets, I discovered empty sachets of Solpadeine, broken pills and strings of used dental floss. I ran my fingers along its frayed edges. Crusted with toothpaste and Shavex, the material was still warm and damp from his morning shower.

There were times when Abba would come to sleep with me in my bed at night when I was eight or nine years old. Why? I never knew, but it didn't really matter. Sometimes he slept, and sometimes he'd just lie awake, no doubt listening to the shouts of revellers leaving the Leinster pub up the road. Often, I'd hug his back, the threadbare feeling of his dressing gown on my cheek and listen to his heart beating like a metronome. After a few minutes he'd go back to his room, leaving me alone.

Abba refused to replace his tatty dressing gown, claiming there was nothing wrong with it. No one could see the stains and holes he'd say, and he'd only have to go back to Marks and Spencer's, a store he hated, to buy a new one. And they didn't make them like they used to. This piece of material seemed to matter as much to him as his greying handkerchiefs. He kept one in the pocket of every pair of trousers he owned, and would use them to blow his nose, wipe up food spills and dust books. I considered leaving his dressing gown for Ines to discard but didn't want him to be cold at home without it, so I stuffed it into his suitcase.

The books he'd brought were stacked on his bedside table. I picked up *Everyman*, felt the creases of its spine and flicked through the pages with my thumb, filling the air with a musty smell as the type fluttered in my eyes. On the inside cover, I noticed Abba's signature and date of purchase in twisted, almost illegible handwriting. He signed every book he bought.

"Aren't you taking these?" I asked as I joined him on the balcony.

Abba squinted in the glare. "I thought Steinberg might like them. What's his name could give them to him."

"You mean Richard?"

"Yeh, that fella."

"I thought he said he didn't read much?"

"So? I'd like him to have them, so we can discuss them next time we meet."

"You don't need to see him again, do you?"

"You never know."

"You never lend anyone your books."

"Didn't I lend you *Herzog*?"

I sat on the balcony for a few minutes, the heat of the winter sun warming my jeans. With the sun in my eyes, I pressed down on my closed eyelids and enjoyed watching multicoloured oil leaks spread in my vision. An aeroplane flew low overhead, punching a hole in the clouds as it sucked the air, shattering the silence. I thought of bringing up our chat from the night before. Parts of it lingered in my mind like a play I could only remember bits of. Was I the one that was meant to apologise? Should I say something? But every time I tried to talk, hoping the right words would just come out, all I could think of was the scrunched up piece of paper I'd discarded with the carcass of the lobster among the cigarette ash and garlic butter. Was that it?

"Come on," I said, holding his books.

"What's the rush?"

"You know I don't like being late."

A smell of diesel fumes filled the hotel lobby as airport coaches lined up outside, air conditioning on full blast, exhausts dripping. Families huddled for one last photo in front of the pool, and a group of lads were knocking back brunch-time pints in the bar. Our suitcases rhythmically click-clacked over the marble tiles as we walked towards the exit.

"Oh, Lewis," Mrs O'Dwyer's shrill voice rang across the lobby.

Shit, the O'Dwyers.

"Lewis, Lewis." Her diminutive frame ran after us.

Abba and I stopped and turned.

She took a moment to catch her breath and puffed twice from

a Ventolin inhaler she retrieved from her bag.

"Are you OK Maureen?" asked Tom, who ran up alongside her, lakes of sweat saturating the underarms of his souvenir t-shirt.

"Lewis, I'm so glad we caught you," she said.

"Hello again," Abba said.

"I wanted to let you know that, well, after our conversation the other night, Tom and I have decided to return to the Holy Land later this year. You," she said, pointing at Abba, "convinced us it was a great idea." Her voice rose an octave. "And we thought you should join us. It's just, you are so knowledgeable about Israel, and I think you said that you speak the language, so that will be very useful. What do you say?" She looked up eagerly at Abba.

"I'd love to, but—"

"No buts now Lewis," she interrupted. "Think about it, we could fly together, the three of us, and if you like, you could bring your son too. Our number is here in case you'd like to talk it over." She stuffed a piece of paper into Abba's hand.

"Thank you."

"Call me Maureen. Oh, by the way, did you get the note we left under your door yesterday inviting you for a last night after-dinner drinkey?" she asked.

"I didn't see a note," I interrupted.

"Oh, that's strange. Richard assured us it was room 304, didn't he Tom?"

Tom nodded.

"The cleaner must have tidied it away," I coughed. "We really have to get going now, we've a flight to catch." I tried to get Abba to move.

"Well, I'm sure there'll be another time. Maybe next year, in

Bethlehem," she proclaimed.

"Or Tenerife," Abba said.

I exchanged a bemused look with Tom.

"Excuse me one moment." Abba shook their hands and shuffled his way to the bathroom.

"Bye now," she called and waved after him. "And you." She stared at me. "Look after him."

The crowd in the lobby thickened. I stood over our suitcases waiting for Abba's return, and watched Joe run past me towards the exit, dragging his hold-all along the ground behind him.

"You off?" It was Richard.

We'd never get to the car at this rate.

"I was going to put the stuff in the car and then say goodbye."

"No you weren't."

"I was."

"I know what you and your dad are like. You were just going to sneak off."

"I wasn't."

"Busted, you liar! Does your dad want a quick one for the road?"

"I think he's had enough this week, don't you? Oh, I almost forgot. My father asked if you could give these to Doctor Steinberg." I handed him the Roth and Zweig.

"Deadly."

"They are," I said.

Richard looked confused. "I'll give them to him next time someone fakes a heart attack," he laughed.

"Very funny."

"You do realise your dad isn't wearing any shoes," Richard said, pointing at Abba as he ran off to help someone who was straining to lift a bloated suitcase onto a trolley.

"Shit," I muttered. "Abba, where are your sandals?" I whispered as he returned from the bathroom.

"I can't wear them. The rubber makes my feet sweat."

"But you can't walk around in bare feet."

"For the life of me I don't know why anyone would want to make sandals out of rubber. There was nothing wrong with my old leather pair that your mother insisted on throwing away. They lasted me for twenty years. I bought them in the Old City in Jerusalem. Marvellous they were." He paused. "While you're here, help me with some of this will you?" He handed me a tube of foot cream.

We sat on the edge of the water fountain in the hotel lobby. I helped Abba raise his feet onto my lap. He sat up straight as I massaged the thick emollient into his swollen feet as if I was some kind of hired help. Working one foot at a time, I massaged the cracked skin between his toes, loosened the taut muscles of his ankles and softened his calloused heels. As I worked, my face red and hot, I noticed a few teenagers around us. They sniggered, and one of them buried her head into her friend's shoulder. I glared at them until they scurried away giggling.

"Can you do my feet now?" Richard asked as he returned.

I raised my eyebrows.

"I have something for you."

He dug into a plastic bag and removed a t-shirt that he held in front of my chest. 'Richie's Famous Mid-Week Pub Crawl' was emblazoned in yellow block letters on the front around a photo of a grinning Richard in the middle. "Thought you might like it, as a souvenir."

"That's, eh, lovely."

"Aren't you going to try it on?"

"I'll try it on later."

"Well, let me know if it doesn't fit. I can always send you another size," he said.

I smiled at him.

"OK then... eh, come and see us, you know, next time you visit."

As I stood up from putting Richard's t-shirt in my bag, the blood drained from my head, leaving me light-headed for a moment. I raised my eyes to look at Richard and wondered if I should shake his hand, hug him, or punch him lightly on the shoulder. At that moment he felt like the only friend I had.

He tightened the Velcro strap of his Fila visor and stuffed his hands into the pockets of his shorts. "Listen, I've got to go. Airport coach duties call. See you later." He held up the palm of his hand, turned on the heels of his Converse boots and walked away.

"See yeh," I called after him, the words catching in my throat.

Abba and I walked across the gravelly car park, sweat dripping into my eyes as I dragged both suitcases over the uneven surface.

As I drove out of the car park, the Cinquecento bouncing over potholes, I turned on the spray and windscreen wipers to clean a layer of dust that blanketed the car. Maybe I'd catch a glimpse, or a wave from Richard, or Harold and Jürgen, or Ines, or Raul, or Joe, or Dr Steinberg, or Mr and Mrs O'Dwyer between the coaches and the crowds, but they'd all disappeared. Once again, Abba and I were alone.

We drove along a dual carriageway towards Reina Sophia Airport which took us around the edges of the national park. The distant sugary peak of Volcan Teide disappeared into thin clouds in my rearview mirror. It felt strange driving past Bodega Ruiz, the vista with the cross, and the sign to La Caleta knowing we wouldn't be visiting them again. I wasn't one for going back to the same place twice, but I noted where the turnings and road signs were, just in case I returned.

I lit a cigarette and flicked the ash out of a narrow opening in the window. Every so often I'd drop a gear and accelerate close enough to a coach in front so that I could read the registration plate, indicate, and edge out to see if I could pass. The slick movement of the car drifting to the other side of the road felt dangerously calming.

"How are you doing financially?" Abba asked, tapping his fingers on the door rest.

I pretended not to hear.

"It's a simple enough question."

"Why do you ask?"

"I'd like to know."

"I suppose I'm doing OK. Shit," I said. Lights flashed at me from the other direction as I tried to pass a coach.

"Have you worked out your monthly outgoings?"

"I think so…"

"It's important that you do," he continued. "And pension, have you thought about that? My financial advisor's marvellous.

Let me know if you need their help, will you? Do you have life insurance?"

Where was this coming from?

"We do," he continued, "worth every penny or cent, or whatever it's called these days. Believe me, you don't want to leave your life in the hands of what you might get from the bloody government. Get some insurance, you hear me? You never know when you might, you know..."

"What?"

"Look, you won't regret it."

"Why are you telling me this?"

"Isn't this what I should be doing? Giving you advice. Isn't that what you wanted?"

"No. I mean yes."

"Well, there you are. If you need my help, you know where I am."

"Yeh," I said quietly, "thanks."

"Pull over, will you?"

I stopped the car at lay-by so that Abba could pee. As he relieved himself, drops of urine jumped from his puddle of piss, spotting his dusty feet.

Through a clump of olive trees in the distance I saw what looked like a tall sculpture of a naked woman. I walked for a couple of minutes along the side of the road to get a closer look and entered an untidy garden through a metal gate that creaked like a grinding brake.

The garden looked as if a bomb had exploded in a modern art gallery. A white stone sculpture of a naked woman with a bulging pregnant belly and one breast stood in the centre of the space on a stone plinth. Around her, roughly painted wooden totem poles speared into the sky. Scattered elsewhere were dolls wearing wigs, shoes half-painted in luminous colours dangling on tree branches by their laces and the frames of rusty discarded prams. The shaved bark of eucalyptus trees covered the ground like pencil shavings, and bloated succulents dotted the volcanic earth.

Cracked mirrors with mosaic frames had been placed opposite some of the bigger pieces. Standing in front of one of the mirrors I noticed my reflection. After a week away, my beard was thicker, my face fuller, my forearms tanned. I shifted my weight onto one leg and then the other, and tried to straighten my back, but was unable to get a clear view of my reflection in the mottled glass, as if half of me had been left behind.

The garden was a couple of hundred metres from the road, but the hum of the traffic was still audible. Next to the garden was a low white cottage with an open door. Maybe I was trespassing, but I needed to get a closer look. Approaching the house, my heart jumped as I spotted the clothed body of an elderly man wearing a yellow woollen jumper and jeans lying on the ground. His trainers pointed towards the sky. He had a curled long moustache. His eyes were closed. His breath was slow and calm. For a brief moment I saw what Abba yearned for; a moment of peace and quiet in his own space, a closeness to the earth, surrounded by his work and belongings. I was tempted to lie down next to the man and fall asleep, content with being among the silence and incompleteness of this hidden world.

Perhaps the man was putting on his own show by lying down and ignoring roaming visitors or maybe this was his daily routine.

But either way I felt calm at the thought that he was there and whatever else was going on around him was of little consequence to him and that was enough. He had found his peace.

I was afraid I'd disturb his contentedness, so I tip-toed back to the sculpture of the pregnant woman for one final look, trying not to crunch the bark under my feet. Standing next to her, I admired her beauty and scale, felt the curves of her form, the smoothness of the cold stone in my hand, and the hollow sound of the sea when I put my ear to her plinth. Her pull urged me to stay, but I remembered that we had a flight to catch, so I walked back to the car, blinking as a wind swept some dust into my eyes.

The 12:40 flight from Tenerife to Dublin was delayed. Abba and I sat in a bar reading and drinking coffees. Around us, passengers rested their heads on tables and lay on the floor, using their luggage to support their backs. Suitcases surrounded us, some wrapped in cellophane, others with zips bulging from the weight of belongings. A low burble came from a television behind the bar. Waiters chatted as they served drinks and washed glasses, and travellers spoke on mobile phones giving updates on departure times. I turned the pages of *Herzog* quickly, skipping sentences, and every now and again, calculating just how many more pages I had to read.

"You nearly finished?" Abba asked, looking up from *The Slave*.

"Just about."

"Enjoying it?"

"It's getting better. I just found the first half, you know, a bit self-indulgent."

"Self-indulgent?"

"I don't know, maybe all the letter writing, it gets a bit, you know, repetitive. It doesn't really get him anywhere, does it?"

"Doesn't it?"

"Well not yet anyway."

"Wait and see. Don't be in such a rush to find out what happens."

"I'm not."

"You are, I can see you rushing. Slow down."

I put *Herzog* down and checked my text messages to see if anyone had been in touch since I'd been away. Nothing. A father and his son sat next to us playing a game on a Nintendo. They furiously thumbed the buttons on the controls, desperately trying to get balls to land into imaginary holes and animals to jump onto moving platforms. The boy squealed every time he succeeded in mastering a level, and the father tensed his body back against his chair, a focused look on his face. Every so often the screen would flash up with stars, points and trophies. They'd pause, breathe and start again. I watched them for a few minutes, a look of lost delight on their faces.

"No one writes me anymore. You used to write me, do you remember?" Abba asked.

"Did I?"

"Yes, from all your trips. You wrote great tales of where you'd been and who you'd met and what you'd eaten. Always a great man for remembering what food you had." He smiled.

"I can't even remember what I did yesterday."

"That happens."

I returned to *Herzog*.

181

After a few minutes, Abba looked at his watch, put *The Slave* face down on the table and placed his coffee cup onto its saucer. "Maybe I'll write you from here one day," he mused.

"Write to me? From here?" I looked at him over my glasses, only half-concentrating.

"Yes."

"You mean, next time you come here on holiday."

"No, I mean write you, from here."

"You've lost me. We are here. What do you mean? Send me a postcard?"

"Aren't you listening? Write you, from here," Abba said slowly. "Once I get settled in that is, tell you all about it."

"All about what?"

"Everything. Who I meet, what I eat, what I read." He raised his eyebrows.

"Ha, ha, very funny," I said, looking up at the departures screen. "Gate 42. Come on, our flight's been called."

Abba held his hands together. I noticed they weren't shaking. "Lis-ten, I'm not joking, I've decided to stay. Here. In Tenerife," he spoke quietly.

I laughed loudly, startling the people next to us. I quickly realised though that Abba wasn't joining in, so straightened my smile. "Come on, let's go. I promised Imma I'd deliver you home safely," I said.

She was expecting Abba back home that evening, around seven o'clock. We'd agreed that I'd exit the airport and put him in a taxi before catching my flight back to London. I'd booked the airport buggy to get us through arrivals so he wouldn't have to walk, and I'd be there to help him with his suitcase. Thirty

182

euros would cover the taxi, and I was to call her when he was safely in the cab. It would be cold, so I was to make sure that he didn't spend too long waiting outside in the rain, and even though his feet were hot and painful, he had to wear some socks, otherwise he'd catch a cold and, well, that could go on for weeks and next thing you know he'd have a chest infection. Also, he had to go to the toilet before he left the airport. I was to remind him to get on and book his next trip to London and to not leave it too long. It would be good for him to spend some time with me, rather than for him to hold court at home, waiting for me to return. He had to take his Insulin before he got home, so they could eat dinner quickly, watch the news and go to bed. He'll need an early night after the flight and my mother had things to do, and she didn't want him to get too tired. If he had time, he was to try to phone Mr Stein from the Jewish Museum so that he could confirm the date and time of his Joyce talk, but if not, that was also OK, it could wait. He could do it the next day.

"I'm not going home," he said.

"What do you mean, 'I'm not going home'?"

"I've arranged to stay in the hotel for a while."

"What do you mean, 'for a while'?"

"What's his name and I organised it yesterday when you were off doing the laundry. He gave me an excellent deal, threw in some meals and a free glass of wine every night. Bit stingy if you ask me, but he said it was the best he could do."

"What? Richard? Why would he do that? Why didn't he tell me?"

"Because I asked him not to."

"I thought we were friends. He gave me a bloody t-shirt," I said angrily.

"I didn't want you to find out from him, OK?"

"Oh, that's nice of you. You brought me all the way here, so you could drop this bombshell."

"I wanted to see you off."

"Great, so I'm supposed to just get on the plane alone, am I?"

"You'll be fine," he said. "Look, if you're worried about the flight, take half a Valium." He dug into the pocket of his smock, burst a pill from a foil packet and snapped it in two with his teeth. "Here." He placed it in the palm of his hand.

"I don't want any of your fucking pills." I knocked the pill out of his hand. "I want you to come home, with me."

"Don't get angry."

"I'm not angry!"

"Flight 275 to Dublin, gate 42," a tannoy announced.

"Come on, joke's over," I said nervously.

"I told you. I'm not going. I'm staying." Abba looked at me seriously. "What's his name said he'd collect me once you'd gone, that's if I ever manage to work out how to use this phone." He removed his Nokia mobile phone from the pocket of his smock and placed it on the table.

"Jesus, you don't even know his name. It's Richard!"

"I know it's Richard."

"You can't just stay here, what will you do?"

"Lie in the sun. Read. There's plenty to do. I might sample a few more restaurants, I don't know…"

"That's just it, you don't know. You'll be bored with no one to entertain you, no one for you to moan at, no one to help you.

Who will take you to the doctors? Who will cook for you? Who will take you to the beach? Who will massage your bloody feet? Who will you talk to? For God's sake!"

Abba often recounted his dream of living once again in the countryside. For a few years in his twenties, he rented a one bedroom apartment that was part of an Edwardian house on the coastal Vico Road in Bray in south county Dublin. Sash windows looked out onto the Irish Sea that battered the shoreline. Abba lived there before I was born, but he talked about it romantically, his escape from the world. A few grainy black and white slides survive portraying him living in that house. He used to show them at one of his slide shows. "Oh, here I am," he'd say, as we watched photos of him posing in a wicker chair reading or standing in front of his gramophone changing records or frying a steak at the stove. I feared that this was what he thought life would be like in the hotel. But maybe, like me, he had to find out for himself.

"I'll be fine, I'll manage," he said. "And so will you."

"Yeh right, you'll be hassling Steinberg every day. Is that what this is about?" I furiously searched in my backpack for our boarding cards.

"I just feel like staying in the sun. I need it. I only have a few years left you know…"

"But you said yourself that the heat makes you tired."

"Everything makes me tired my son."

The tinkle of the father and son's video game got louder.

"Last time I checked, I'm allowed to do what I want, aren't I?"

"No, you're not just allowed. What about your friends, your family? What about Imma? What about me?"

"What about you?"

"Do you expect me to come and visit you every few months?"

"That would be nice, and I'm sure Richard would like to see you. You can go on one of his crawls, or whatever they're called."

"When did you decide?" I asked.

"The other day."

"And what will I say to Imma?"

"Tell her I'll call. She'll understand. She doesn't want me there anyway."

"That's not fair."

"Really? She's said so many times that I should do what I want, so, there you go, I'm doing it. Isn't that what you all wanted? To get rid of me."

"I didn't want to get rid of you."

"Don't think I didn't understand what you were all saying in Hebrew about me behind my back."

"We didn't—"

"It's in the past," he interrupted, "I don't blame you. Perhaps I wasn't the easiest person to live with."

"Abba, come on, stop it," I said. "Please just... stop it, you've made your point. We're going. Now."

Picking up both of our bags I stumbled over bodies and luggage and charged towards the security gate. As I took my place at the back of the snaking queue, I tried to inhale deeply, but my lungs tightened. I was moving, but languidly, like a rag doll. I looked around to see where he was through the crowd of people. He was still at the bar. I dropped our bags, excused my way through the crowd and ran back to him.

"I need you to come. Now. We'll miss our flight," I said

forcefully, grabbing Abba's shoulders. I tried to move him, but his trunk stayed solid and still. Abba placed his hands over mine, the warmth of his hold softening my grasp. One by one, he unravelled my fingers and let my arms drop by my side. He held my hands, his skin rough and dry, like the material of his dressing gown.

"Final call, flight 275 to Dublin, gate 42."

My head hurt from all the extra things I wanted to say, but I couldn't find the words. I knew at that moment that this was how it was going to end. I wondered if I'd ever see him again. Would he die here, alone on this island, surrounded by volcanic rock and empty bottles of red wine? The thought crossed my mind that his plan was to do just that. Next time I'd see him, he'd be in a box in his dressing gown, a couple of books by his side. Maybe he was right after all. Maybe he didn't have much else to live for. It annoyed me though that he was probably right. I never wanted to admit it, but he always seemed to know the right answers. He'd been planning this all along and I never knew, but he knew. And for a moment, I felt that I should be the one to stay with him. I didn't have much else to do. I could find a job, work with Richard, maybe as a lifeguard. Do the things I wanted to do. But something held me back. Despite everything, I was still the quiet one. The diplomat. The maestro who didn't play. This was his story. He didn't need me here. I knew he wanted to be alone. I had to let him go. For him as well as for me.

"Off you go now," he said.

I felt like a child being sent to school on my first day.

"Come and visit, anytime you want. I'll save you a drink at the bar, how about that?"

Reluctantly I let go of Abba's hands and held his face in my palms for a few moments, feeling his prickly stubble and rubbing a shaving nick on his chin with my thumb. I waited for tears to come, but they didn't. A beam of soft sunlight shone onto our faces, and as we looked at each other time slowed, and for a few seconds, everything was motionless and clear.

I unzipped the front section of his suitcase and removed his sandals. Kneeling on the floor, his hand resting on my head, I helped him raise one foot after the other into his rubber shoes and stretched the Velcro tight over the tops of his feet. I stood up slowly, rubbing my head into his body, taking in his familiar odour. His cheeks were rested and plump, his forehead was loose, and his chin sagged under his mouth. He didn't feel or scratch his hernia, and his hands weren't shaking but resting, at ease, in mine. After a few moments, he gradually let his fingers go from my grasp.

"Write me," he said.

I nodded, picked up my suitcase and re-joined the queue.

I sat in Abba's aisle seat on the aeroplane and left the middle seat empty. The seat felt sticky, and the floor was littered with crumbs from the previous flight. I was handed a well-thumbed in-flight magazine advertising meal deals, chocolate, crisps, beer and fizzy drinks and souvenirs. Lottery scratch cards were on offer this month, twelve for ten euro, a chance to win a million. I thought of buying a handful. Did anyone ever win these prizes? A million euro would be nice. Enough to buy Abba a beach house in Tenerife so he wouldn't have to stay in the Hotel Optimist, and for me to visit, maybe once or twice a year.

The heat of the aeroplane was stifling. Passengers fanned themselves with menu cards, and I fiddled with the air vent that blew warm air onto my head. What would I say to my mother? He decided to stay. Of course I tried to change his mind and told him that he was being ridiculous, but you know what he's like. No, he didn't discuss it with me. I've no idea if he'd planned it. I don't think it was the reason he went on holiday, at least not as far as I know. Did he say anything to you? He just sprung it on me. At the airport. As we were waiting for the gate to be announced. I practically pushed him towards departures, but he refused. I wasn't going to get aggressive with him. God knows how that might have ended. What else could I do? He didn't move. Said the Holiday Rep, Richard, was going to collect him. He's planning on staying in the hotel for a while and then decide what he wants to do. I've no idea what he's going to do. You know what he's like. He needs constant entertaining. We found a doctor the other day, so at least he has someone to talk to. Why? Because he didn't take enough Insulin with him. I'm sure you counted it correctly. No one is blaming you. And we had to go to the hospital one day. No, he's fine, it was the usual panic about his heart. Why didn't I tell you? There was nothing to tell. There's nothing wrong with him, as per usual. The same doctor saw him. Yes. He said he'd call in a few days and tell us how he's getting on. That's if he works out how to charge and turn on his phone. I'm not sure it even works over there. Mind you, we can always call him at the hotel. I have the number somewhere. I think Richard will look out for him. I don't see why you can't call him now. It's the same time zone, so he's probably having dinner. No, the food at the hotel is a bit dry, but I'm not sure where else he's going to eat as you have to drive to all the other decent places we went to, and there's no way he should drive on those roads. I thought he was having a good time. Yeh, we got on fine. Yes, fine. I give him a week, maybe two. He'll get bored of being alone.

The empty seat rattled as the aeroplane sped down the runway into the crisp blue sky. As it dipped its right wing, I could clearly see the rocky, sand shoreline of the island, black like a burnt crust around its edge. High-rise hotels dotted the coast, swimming pools sparkled in the sun, and cars looked toy-like as they zipped along the roads. Climbing higher above the clouds, I gripped the armrests of the seat and held my breath as a burst of turbulence shook the aeroplane. The woman sitting by the window held her hand over her mouth and looked over at me for reassurance as we bounced in our seats.

An eerie chill came over me that I'd left something behind. I half expected Abba to return at any moment from the bathroom, knock my knees with his legs as he'd struggle into his seat, take *The Slave* from the pocket of his smock and start reading. He'd doze for a few minutes, demand a drink, go to the toilet again, doze some more and read. My hand smoothed the plastic of the empty seat, my skin tingling for the warmth of his hand. I brushed a few more crumbs onto the floor, lifted the clasp and buckled the spare seat belt, doing it up tight, just in case. The woman who was now resting her forehead against the window, briefly turned her head to me and raised her eyebrows. Patting the seat I smiled at her, as if nothing was wrong.

"Sir, anything to drink?" a flight attendant asked as the drinks trolley brushed my leg.

"Do you have any whiskey?" I asked.

"Yes, we have Bullseye."

"I'll have two please, with a glass. No ice."

"Any scratch cards?"

I shook my head. Ripping open the sachets of Bullseye with my teeth, I poured the whiskey into the plastic glass, un-clicked the tray table in front of Abba's seat and placed the glass in the cup holder. I folded a paper napkin and placed it next to the glass in case of any spillages. Everything was ready for his return. He'd only be a few more minutes.

As the aeroplane levelled out, I took off my sandals and socks and stretched out my feet. I opened *Herzog*. The pages were dog-eared and stained from the pool water, bits of sand fell from between the pages. I sipped some of Abba's whiskey while I carefully read every word of the last few pages, swishing the harsh alcohol around my mouth, warming the back of my throat. I fixed my gaze onto the print so as not to miss anything in case Abba asked me any questions. By the end, the main character, Moses Herzog, stops writing letters, realising that he has nothing left to say and just wants some quiet. The gripes, arguments and frustrations that filled his life seemed to have been quelled.

Abba himself was never much of a letter writer but for a short period when I was at university in the early 1990s, he wrote me a couple of letters. Printed on his Olivetti Dot Matrix printer, they were full of typos. For a brief time he was at ease. He joked about what pieces of his clothing my mother had thrown away, how much he hated travelling to London, and why I should always call him for love life advice. There'd be stories about injuries from carving meat, plays he had to study and the "twaddle" that was broadcast on RTÉ. I looked forward to receiving those letters and devoured every word, the rough feeling of the paper, the twists of his signature, always written with a fountain pen, the indecipherable address on the envelope. But after a while the letters stopped. I don't know why. I missed them. I hoped that Abba would start writing to me again with his news from the Hotel Optimist. I could picture him sitting on the balcony of his apartment in his dressing gown, or by the pool in his swimming trunks, a whiskey always in hand. His head would be turned towards the sun, and he'd close his eyes every few moments and let the heat warm his ageing skin. Roth or Zweig or Bashevis-Singer would be by his side. If he did, I'd memorise every word, feel the thin edges of the paper with my fingers, and smell the dried ink, the stamp, the glue from the envelope.

I closed *Herzog*, rested it on my lap and waited. Abba would be back in a minute. I'd show him that I'd finished.

"Ahhh, finally, you listened to me. You persevered. It's marvellous, don't you think?" he'd ask.

Yes, it was.

…I have no doubt that when I next see you, you will be a changed man, but then that's what life is all about. Do I have to tell you how much I love you? Well why not… of course I do. So goodbye!

Lots of love,

Louis, Abba, Lentz, Lewis, Dad, Loucho and no doubt many others…

ACKNOWLEDGEMENTS

This book is about my father, Louis Lentin who died in July 2014. He was a wonderful man; creative, bright, witty, funny, stubborn and very loving. He was also someone who made change happen. Through his work he asked difficult and uncomfortable questions that many people often didn't like but had to be asked. He had an unnerving ability to get under the skin of things. He never asked for plaudits, was often shy about his successes, and always believed that no one would remember him when he died. Well, he is remembered, loved and not forgotten by many.

I am immensely grateful to my mother and sister for their support in publishing this book. To Goran Baba Ali, my publisher, who I met while we did our MAs in Creative Writing and have remained friends ever since, my editor Jessica Sanchez who perfected my imperfections, and Partho Sen-Gupta and Nil Müge Felekten who designed the cover, thank you, you are all wonderful.

To Arielle, Eden, and Miriam, I love you.

"I enjoyed this very much. The situation and location added a wonderfully strange atmosphere. By making his story very specifically Jewish/Irish, Lentin actually releases its universal quality. Everything about the characters and their relationship feels recognisable and true for sons and fathers everywhere. There will be no final answers. Beautifully achieved."

Gerry Stembridge, author of *The Effect of Her*, *Ordinary Decent Criminal* and the film *Nora*

"*Winter Sun* is a candid, sometimes darkly humorous book, about a man who goes on holiday with his elderly father to Tenerife. A clever portrait of a stormy but ultimately loving relationship between father and son, the story falls somewhere between novel and memoir, exploring themes of loss and identity through beautiful prose, with moments of sharp wit and insight. *Winter Sun* will no doubt speak to fathers and sons everywhere – an engrossing read, with lots of heart!"

Jane Labous, author of *Past Participle*

"*Winter Sun* by Miki Lentin is a captivating debut novel exploring father and son relationships, love, loss, hope, and the human condition during a week the writer spends with his aging father. Lentin's writing style is impactful, and it evokes a range of emotions in the reader. The book's ten chapters are beautifully written, each with a unique and thought-provoking message. Overall, *Winter Sun* is an emotionally engaging story that is definitely worth checking out."

Nizan Weisman, author of *Rosemary Woods* and *A Place*, shortlisted for Israel's Sapir Prize

Also by Afsana Press:

Inner Core

Short stories by Miki Lentin

Death, anxiety, masculinity, family and children, social good and rocks. All things that touch the life of a middle-aged man. Miki Lentin goes in search of a rock with his child in Ireland, travels to Istanbul with his wife while sleep-deprived, recounts memories of working and growing up in Dublin and explores what it means to do good in society today. *Inner Core* portrays, in a minimalist tone, Lentin's life on the edge.

'..sensitively observed and moving.'
Daniel Trilling, author of *Lights in the Distance*

'Lentin takes linear time and smashes it to pieces, reassembling the shards as narrative mosaics.'
Lynda Clark, author of *Dreaming in Quantum*

Release date: April 2022 / 168 pages
Paperback: £ 7.99 / ISBN: 9781739982447
E-Book: £ 5.99 / ISBN: 9781739982430

The Glass Wall

A novel by Goran Baba Ali

The tale of a teenage refugee who must re-live the pain of his past to enter a land waiting behind a glass wall. Will his story be convincing enough to guarantee his safety? A story of struggle and persecution, yet abundant in hope, *The Glass Wall* is a clear-eyed, emotionally honest account of displaced people, illustrating the true hardship that refugees experience.

'An unforgettable novel, made cruelly relevant by what has been taking place in Europe.'
Neal Ascherson, Writer & Journalist

'Poetic and beautifully rendered, it probes the boundaries between those who have and those who seek.'
Isabel Hilton OBE, Journalist & Broadcaster

Release date: November 2021 / 352 pages
Hardback: £ 14.99 / ISBN: 9781739982409
Paperback: £ 11.99 / ISBN: 9781739982416 (April 2024)

Also by Afsana Press:

Past Participle

A novel by Jane Labous

Dakar, Senegal, 1987: On a rainy night after a wild party, the British ambassador's wife, Vivienne Hughes, is involved in a car crash. Her vehicle hits the motorbike of a young Senegalese doctor, Aimé Tunkara, killing him. Three decades later, Aimé's little sister, Lily Tunkara, now a high-flying lawyer in Dakar, finds a photograph that compels her to investigate what really happened that rainy night.

'*Past Participle* is a captivating story of murder and imperialist corruption, of friendship and motherhood and of the past haunting the present, told through the interlinking stories of two women. The novel tackles an important subject matter, but in a way that doesn't feel hectoring or didactic. It recognises the nuances of power dynamics, personal desires and social and political realities in framing how people act and why. The novel offers a strong critique of western imperialism, attentive to the macro and micro applications of that, alongside a dynamic and moving story.'

Kieran Devaney, Author & Literary Editor

Release date: September 2023 / 352 pages

Paperback: £ 10.99 / ISBN: 9781739982478

Also by Afsana Press:

Whispering Walls

A novel by Choman Hardi

The US invasion of Iraq is looming. Three siblings – two in London, one in Slemany – recall their troubled past. Stories of war, displacement, and coming to terms with the tragedies of a Kurdish family, all told from their different perspectives. Torn between two countries and various life stories, the siblings find themselves dealing with complex life choices, and the mystery of their sister's suicide twenty-two years ago. *Whispering Walls* is a story of love, relationships, affection, and hope, with a cautious view of the future.

'A book that is written with the same sharp observation, fresh language and moral imagination of Hardi's award-winning poetry, it asks a question we all must consider: how can we grapple with the tragedies of the past as we try to fashion a better future? Not only is Choman Hardi a brilliant poet, she is also a great novelist. I want everyone I know to read her book!'

Catherine Davidson, Poet & Novelist

Release date: September 2023 / 304 pages
Paperback: £ 10.99 / ISBN: 9781739982454